D1515864

BLOW BY BLOW . . .

Remo hit. A shoulder groaned in its socket, shattered, and fell away from his fist. Without a second's hesitation, the Dutchman's other arm lashed out and took Remo in the ribs. Two sharp snaps sent Remo back, reeling. An inch closer, and they would have pierced his heart.

Then another shape loomed nearby. Instinctively, Remo charged for it before realizing it was Chiun. He stopped cold and Chiun spoke.

"Move!" the old man said. But Remo moved too late. Chiun's tiny figure in the mist upended and seemed to blow away in the wind.

"Chiun!" Remo called.

Silence.

"Chiun!"

The hand came out of nowhere toward Remo's temple.

"Chiun," he whispered as the walls of consciousness came crashing in blackness around him. It had been a glancing blow, but enough to stop Remo. Enough to weaken him. The next would kill him. He was beaten.

THE DESTROYER SERIES:

ATTENTION: SCHOOLS AND CORPORATIONS
PINNACLE Books are available at quantity discounts with bulk purchases for educational, business or special promotional use. For further details, please write to: SPECIAL SALES MANAGER, Pinnacle Books, Inc., 1430 Broadway, New York, NY 10018.

WRITE FOR OUR FREE CATALOG

If there is a Pinnacle Book you want—and you cannot find it locally—it is available from us simply by sending the title and price plus 75¢ to cover mailing and handling costs to:

Pinnacle Books, Inc.
Reader Service Department
1430 Broadway
New York, NY 10018

Please allow 6 weeks for delivery.
___Check here if you want to receive our catalog regularly.

The Destroyer #46

NEXT OF KIN

Warren Murphy

PINNACLE BOOKS   NEW YORK

For Dave Slobodin and the House of Sinanju,
Box 1454, Secaucus, N.J. 07094.

This is a work of fiction. All the characters and events portrayed in this book are fictional, and any resemblance to real people or incidents is purely coincidental.

THE DESTROYER #46: NEXT OF KIN

Copyright © 1981 by Richard Sapir and Warren Murphy

All rights reserved, including the right to reproduce this book or portions thereof in any form.

An original Pinnacle Books edition, published for the first time anywhere.

First printing, November 1981

ISBN: 0-523-40720-3

Cover illustration by Hector Garrido

Printed in the United States of America

PINNACLE BOOKS, INC.
1430 Broadway
New York, New York 10018

NEXT OF KIN

Prologue

It was known to the natives as Devil's Mountain. The white men on the island were unfamiliar with the name or the mountain, since the ragged lump of volcanic rock straddling the French/Dutch border of Sint Maarten did not reach even half the height of Paradise Peak or any of the other more picturesque and geologically newer mountains in the area.

But the native islanders knew. In the hushed and reverent tones reserved for telling their children the island legends that would be passed on to the next generation, the elders among the hill dwellers spoke of Devil's Mountain and its legacy of death.

It was on Devil's Mountain that the Carib Indians performed their rites of war against invading tribesmen, eating the flesh of their enemies to take their strength. A thousand years before Columbus came to claim the island for Spain, the Caribs squatted along the rim of the already long-dead volcano to toss the gleaming bones of the vanquished into its crater.

And after the Spaniards came, with their muskets and cannons, trying to wipe them off the face of the earth, the Carib Indians assembled on Devil's Mountain to decide their fate. The brave elected to fight the strange and powerful new enemy. The proud killed their wives and children so that they would not be slain by the metal-wearing invaders. But the old, the infirm, and the wise fled to the caves in the hills, where they watched their ancient race plunge toward extinction. And by night they brought the bones and bloodied bodies of their fallen tribesmen to Devil's Mountain to lie for eternity among the spirits of the dead.

In the hills these cautious few waited as the Spanish left and the English came. As the Dutch came, and the Portuguese, and the French. They waited as the island changed hands sixteen times in two hundred years, through the sugar boom and the slavery boom, which changed the island's color from white to black.

And slowly, as the island evolved into the mutual territory of the Dutch and the French, reigning over an African population, the handful of Carib Indians nurtured among the hills in the shadow of Devil's Mountain ventured one by one toward the shore and the towns where they found

2

women among the black-skinned slaves and took them back to the hills.

Their children were strong and wise in the island ways. And after slavery was abolished from the island, they came out of hiding and married among the island's population, now grown into a race of its own with African and European blood and handsome features and strong bodies. The Caribs added their blood to the brew and mellowed it in the tropical sun and lived in peace with their new brothers for the rest of their days.

And so the fiercesome Carib Indians became extinct as a race. But they did not forget Devil's Mountain.

In the latter half of the eighteenth century, a prosperous cloth merchant from Holland sailed to Sint Maarten with a shipload of lumber and carpenters and European stonemasons to build a replica of a tenth-century castle on the mountain that stood between the French and Dutch borders. He chose the mountain because its ancient volcanic lip still protruded four feet high, making it a natural fortification, and because he didn't give a hang whether or not the French thought half the island was theirs. He was Dutch, the island was Dutch, and he would build his castle wherever he wanted. Besides, the French prefect accepted the Dutchman's gift of 1,000 guilders to leave him alone.

He found later that the bribe was unnecessary. No one wanted the mountain. Europeans would visit the Dutchman in his castle, but they could find no guides to take them there. No island cooks would come to the place, no maids to clean it. No messengers, farmers, laborers. The islanders would not touch Devil's Mountain with the soles of their shoes.

So, bitter and lonely, the Dutchman sailed back to Holland, leaving his castle to fall into neglect and decay for more than a hundred years.

Then, amazingly, the castle came alive again. The natives whispered to one another as the helicopters whirred above the plateau of Devil's Mountain and as the team of burros led by a single, silent man made its way up the slope, dragging behind it the bulky furnace that was to heat the place. They gasped in amazement as the small planes at Juliana Airport disgorged their cargoes of dozens of magnificently beautiful women bound by helicopter for Devil's Mountain. And they stared up at the castle with curiosity and dread as they discussed its new occupant. Who would live in such a place, some asked, with its crumbling walls and smell of death and sadness? Only a European, others answered, like the old Dutchman himself.

Some had seen him, walking through the village with the small, silent man who obeyed his orders and talked to him with his hands. He was extraordinarily handsome, the women said, with yellow hair and eyes of ice blue. He walked like a cat. He would be a good lover. Still, there was something odd about him, something too still. He never smiled, and when he walked into a store, where people could see him, his footsteps made no noise on the floorboards. Animals hated him. He could not come within twenty feet of a donkey or a goat without sending the beast into panic. And though he spoke many languages, he never talked except in the briefest of business exchanges. He had no friends. Not even the Europeans on the island knew him.

They called him the Dutchman.

And all feared him. And avoided Devil's Mountain.

One

The Dutchman waited.

On a deep ledge beneath a bank of narrow archer's windows in the castle, he squatted on his haunches like a cat about to spring. He was dressed in an Oriental gi and his feet were bare on the cold stone of the ledge. In the twilight, his golden hair glinted as the island breeze brushed past his face.

Below him, on the Dutch side of the island, spread the immense Soubise Harbor Transportation Corporation with its thousands of tons of cargo packed into truck containers, awaiting the great ships that would heave into Sint Maarten Harbor. Beyond the harbor, on the other side of the castle, the French section of the island formed a steep cliff overlooking the white beach and coral-dappled shallows of the ocean.

The French side was prettier, but the young man who sat so tensely on the window ledge was drawn, day after day, to the sight of the harbor. His harbor, now.

He smiled to himself. His harbor. He had never even visited the place during operational hours. Each day, hundreds of stevedores, shipping agents, transport crew workers, machinery operators, and sailors went to work at the pier to make a sizable fortune for a man they knew only by rumor. Each day, other men in Phillipsburg and Marigot, the Dutch and French capitals of the island, would arrange the business of the day and chart the company's progress. Each day those men would skim off whatever profit they wished for their own uses. They would pay lawyers, make deals, bribe officials, and build splendid houses for themselves and their families. And each month an envelope filled with 5,000 American dollars would be left in a safety deposit box in Marigot's post office.

Most of the senior officials of the company earned far more than $5,000 a month, but that was the Dutchman's stipulation: $5,000, in exchange for never having to be bothered about the Soubise Harbor Transportation Corporation under any circumstances. It was a strange setup, but they could live with it in considerable comfort. And anyway, everyone knew the Dutchman was mad as a hatter, sitting up in his castle year after year, not seeing anyone but that deaf-mute servant of his and those French whores he was always flying in from Paris. They said in the village that the

7

Dutchman didn't eat meat and didn't even have electricity in the castle. They speculated that even the big oil-burning furnace he'd had towed to the place wasn't large enough to heat the medieval fortress on the hill. He'd probably had it installed just for the girls. It didn't take more than $5,000 a month to take care of a crazy young man who didn't even have electricity.

And he waited. Twilight became night, and the workers left the shipyard. The bright lights above the harbor compound went on, illuminating the palm trees outside the shipyard's fence and the calm ocean beyond. The warm trade winds blew stronger now. They smelled of sea and magic. The Dutchman closed his eyes and remembered.

The Dutchman. Who had ever given him that name? Jeremiah Purcell was about as Dutch as a corn fritter. . . .

Corn. It had all begun with *corn*! The Master had told him that many wondrous things come from strange beginnings, but even the Master himself would have been surprised that Jeremiah's extraordinary talent was brought to light by a tub of field corn.

He was eight or nine years old when it happened. The Incident. The First Time. The Beginning. He had come to call *It* by a variety of names, that afternoon in Kentucky when the wheels of his rare and horrifying destiny began to turn.

The family pig was eating corn behind the mountain shack where Jeremiah lived with his parents. He was an only child; his birthing had nearly killed his mother. There were a lot of

8

chores to be done, and looking after the pig was the least enjoyable of them, so Jeremiah was pleased that the pig would buck and snort and roll its eyes insanely whenever he came near the pen.

His father wasn't pleased. Slopping the hog should have been Jeremiah's job.

"What you do to that hog, boy?" his father would ask every day as he emerged filthy and stinking from the pen, collaring Jeremiah so that the stink would be on him, too.

"Nothing, Pa."

And his father would shove him aside and take a swig from the whiskey crock on the porch. "Musta done something. Threw stones at it, something."

"I didn't do nothing, Pa. He just don't like me."

"One a these days I gonna catch you, boy, hear? And I gonna give you a lickin' you won't forget."

The pig was going to get him a licking, Jeremiah knew, whether he did anything to provoke it or not. His father would use any reason to beat the boy for not slopping the hog himself. Damn fat pig, Jeremiah thought as he leaned against the corncrib at a safe distance from the animal. Probably eat anything, eat until it burst. His fingers played at the crinkly dry ears of corn in the crib. Pig food.

And suddenly, he could see it, an image so real, it blocked out all the sights and sounds around him, a picture in his mind more intense with color and texture than anything in reality. The image was of the pig gobbling up corn until it exploded, raining pork chops all over the yard. It was a funny image, but so real that Jeremiah's laughter was more hysterical than mirthful.

At the same time the picture popped into Jeremiah's brain, the pig began to huff and skitter around its pen, drawing toward the trough, where it began to eat voraciously.

"Pig food! Pig food!" Jeremiah shrieked gleefully, and threw two ears of corn into the pen. The pig finished everything in its trough and went for the corn.

"Pig food!" He carried an armload of corn to the pen. The pig reared back on its hind legs, screaming, as he approached, but began gobbling the corn as soon as the boy moved back toward the corncrib, its eyes frenzied and wide.

He brought over four more armfuls. "Eat till you burst, fat pig," Jeremiah whispered, the image in his head still vibrating quietly. The pig snorted and stomped and ate and searched for more food and ate it.

"Till you burst."

And then the pig moaned, a low, keening sound, and sniffed at the half-eaten ear of corn at its feet, and shuddered. It lay its head in the mud, and with a great thump, its massive body followed. The pig kicked twice in the air with its hind legs, panted, moaned, twisted its neck so that its head faced Jeremiah, and died. Its eyes were open. They stared vacantly at the boy. Jeremiah screamed.

Inside the house, his father stumbled off the couch, shaking himself awake and growling,

10

"What'd he do now? Snotty little pup, prob'ly bothering with that hog again."

He had killed it. Through his screams, a part of Jeremiah realized with utter coldness and clarity that he had done something—something with his *mind*—to cause the occurrence in the pigpen.

His father saw the pig, started to drag its immense corpse out of the mud, then stopped.

"I think I'm going to take care of you first," he said. He ran for Jeremiah, but the boy didn't move. He was still thinking of the pig and the strange, unearthly image that had come into his sight, the killing picture. He had seen death, and death had been created.

He hardly felt his father's rough hand grab hold of his arm and whirl him around. Then the big hand headed straight for his face and jolted it back. The sting brought involuntary tears to his eyes. His father hit him again.

"Don't," the boy said, feeling light-headed. The hand came down again, across his eyes.

"Don't!" It was a command. And while the blow struck, Jeremiah's watering blue eyes locked into his father's, and the lights and colors appeared again. But this time there was a sound along with the colors, a hissing, crackling noise mixed with the orange and yellow of . . . his father's hair. . . .

"You're on fire," the boy said, astonished.

His father screamed, a wild, mountain yell, and slapped frantically at the too-orange flames on his too-blue flannel shirt.

11

It's the picture, Jeremiah said to himself. It's not real—yet. He wanted to move—help his father, run away, anything—but he was rooted to the spot. He tried to make the killing picture go away, but he knew it was too late. He couldn't stop.

His mother, alarmed by the screaming, ran onto the porch, a broom in her hand. She dropped the broom, and both her hands flew to her mouth. She was running toward her husband.

"Go away," the boy snapped, but the picture was too strong. With a gasp, she clutched at the place on her skirt where the flames had erupted. His father caught her by the wrist, and they stumbled off together like two giddy dancers engulfed in flame.

It's not real yet. . . .

They were headed for the pond.

It's not real. . . .

Where they drowned.

"Can't nobody rightly say how it happened," Pap Lewis told the woman from the welfare office a week later at the train station. The woman had come to take Jeremiah to Dover City where, she told him, he would live in a place full of other children who'd lost their parents. Pap Lewis had wanted the boy to live with him and his family, but the welfare office said they were too poor to support another child.

Jeremiah waited quietly as the train steamed up to the platform and the woman took the boy's hand. Pap Lewis gave him a pat on the back and hoisted him up the steps into the train.

12

That was the last time Jeremiah saw him, because the train ride to Dover City was the setting for the second incident, the one-in-a-million chance that took Jeremiah Purcell from the ordinary world and thrust him, literally kicking and screaming, onto a new pathway that ended at Devil's Mountain, with the ultimate Master of Death as his guide.

On the train, Jeremiah left the woman from the welfare office to make his way to the lavatory two cars away. The route took him past a bank of sleeper cabins, where a boy not much older than Jeremiah sprawled on the floor with dozens of baseball cards around him. When Jeremiah tried to step around the boy, he accidentally walked over some of the cards. The boy scrambled to his feet with a shout and pushed Jeremiah into the door of one of the sleeper cabins. Jeremiah didn't strike back, since the boy was bigger than he was and, besides, Jeremiah wasn't much of a fighter. But as he watched the boy gather up his baseball cards, one odd, incongruous thought entered his mind and glowed there like a beacon: *Rabbit.*

The boy did look like a rabbit, with his knees bent near his body as he hunched over the floor. Still, the color in the train was so bright. . . .

The boy looked up, his eyes frozen with terror. He abandoned his cards with a sniff. *No*, Jeremiah thought. As the boy bounded away on all fours, Jeremiah ran with all his strength in the other direction.

At the end of the sleeper car, he smashed full force into a man who had emerged from one of

13

the cabins. A witness! Jeremiah looked around wildly to see if others had been standing around while he had turned the boy into a rabbit. There was only this single passenger, dressed in a blue suit like any businessman, whose face was expressionless as Jeremiah disengaged himself and continued running.

But what a face, he thought as he ran cold water over his head in the lavatory. It was the strangest face he had ever seen. A face that was human, and not disfigured, but unlike any face he had ever looked upon. The color, the shape, the features. He had never seen a face that even remotely resembled it. . . .

The man was waiting for Jeremiah when he returned.

The boy didn't acknowledge him, but he knew that the strange man was following him through the cabin. When he arrived back at the welfare lady's side, the stranger sat down opposite them. Jeremiah trembled with fright. But the man opened a newspaper—harmless enough—while the welfare lady slept.

More than an hour passed. Outside, snow was falling in wet, fat flakes that coated the landscape as the train chug-a-chugged slowly through the Kentucky highlands. The boy dozed. Chug-a-chug, chug-a-chug. A hypnotic stillness fell over the car. The snow was falling with a chug-a-chug beat, chug-a-chug and the snow, the bright, white snow, bright and white, too bright, the snow, chug-a-chug . . .

The snow!

Jeremiah snapped awake to the sounds of people shrieking wildly as a storm of whirling snow blew through the train.

"What—what's this?" the welfare lady grumbled as the snow slowed and ceased and disappeared without a trace of moisture. She looked around for the source of the noise, then went back to sleep.

"It isn't even wet," someone called from a distance. And everyone turned and marveled about what could have caused such a mass hallucination, except for Jeremiah, who fought back tears of panic and sorrow and shame because he knew that he had caused it. He felt as if he'd just had a wet dream in front of fifty people, and he knew they would continue. He was a freak, a dangerous, uncontrollable menace who'd be locked up in prison or killed as soon as people found out about him.

He straightened up. What if nobody did find out about him? If he could get away from the welfare lady who was already beginning to snore, perhaps never reach the home in Dover City. . . . If he could live alone in the mountains, no one would ever know. . . .

But someone did know. The strange-looking man with the newspaper was staring straight at him, unsmiling, appraising. He knew. It was all over. He knew.

With a movement so fast that Jeremiah didn't know what was happening, the man lifted him off his seat and clamped his hand over the boy's mouth. He carried him to the sleeper cabin where Jeremiah had first seen him and threw him inside.

Before Jeremiah could get to his feet, the man

15

swatted him across the cabin with the back of his hand. The motion looked effortless, but the boy felt as though all his bones were broken.

"If you scream, I'll kill you," he said.

He walked in a slow circle around the whimpering child. For several minutes he paced in silence. Then he said, "You are a most exceptional child." He spoke elegantly, unlike the rough Southern mountain twang Jeremiah's ears were accustomed to.

"Where are you going on this train?" the stranger asked.

"Dover City."

"Is that woman your mother?" He inclined his head in the direction of the passenger car.

"No. My parents are dead." He burst into tears. "I killed them."

The man's eyelids lowered and the corners of his mouth curved upward. "Good," he said softly. "Does anyone know what you can do?"

Jeremiah stammered, confused.

"The snow. The boy in the corridor. Things like that."

The boy shook his head.

"You know, if anyone finds out about you, they'll kill you."

Jeremiah's trembling worsened. "I won't do it anymore," he said weakly.

The man laughed. "You know as well as I that you can't control this—this ability of yours. You were asleep when you caused the snowstorm. Stop that sniffling at once." He shoved the boy's shoulder painfully. "It can only be directed. And used.

16

Yes, this talent of yours could prove to be quite helpful."

"At the home in Dover City, they're going to put me in jail, aren't they?"

The man smiled a sly, oily smile. "But you're never going to reach Dover City," he said. "This encounter with me has changed your fate finally and inexorably. You will be rich. You will be free to take anything you want on the face of the earth. You will lead a life that is both unique and invincible. And you will be, with proper guidance and discipline, of invaluable assistance to me."

"Who are you?" the boy asked, ignorant of half the words the strange man had spoken.

"I am the Master," he said.

Then he shattered the glass in the cabin's window, gathered the boy up in his arms, and hurled them both outside into the cold to roll down the snowy, bramble-coated hillside as the train coughed on and out of sight.

Outside the castle's slit windows, the sea rumbled close to the palm trees. High tide. The Dutchman had been in the same position for hours. Waiting. A stranger from the outside would have thought he was resting, but the Dutchman never rested. He waited, and that was different.

The door opened with a soft knock and a squat, dark-haired man wearing a shabby seafarer's uniform entered carrying a red lacquer box.

"What's this for?" the Dutchman asked.

The mute stared at him intently, watching the shape of his lips. He handed the Dutchman the

17

box with a slight bow, then gestured with practiced, fluttering hands a message that made the Dutchman shudder to the tips of his fingers. "It can't be true," he said as the mute drew a long beard in the air. Two men—a tall young white man and an aged Oriental. The mute bowed again, picked up a quill pen and a sheet of rice paper from a table in the room, and wrote with large, difficult strokes:

THEY HAVE COME.

He handed the Dutchman the paper, bowed again, and left the room, again sheathed in darkness except for the eerie light of the full tropical moon outside. The Dutchman looked at the lacquer box in his hands and willed his fingers to stop trembling. When they steadied, he tossed the box into the air, thrust his right hand upward, and with a delicate dancing rhythm of his fingers, shattered the box in midair into a thousand pieces.

An envelope fluttered from its place in the box, where it had rested for many years, and drifted into the Dutchman's hands.

"At last," he said quietly, clutching the envelope to his chest. He rose, feeling the chains of a lifetime loosen and break. He walked to the door, handed the envelope to the mute waiting outside, and said, "Take this to the man called Chiun."

When his servant had disappeared into the night, the Dutchman walked through the castle into a room with a hidden panel that led to another room, a tiny, square black box occupied by a small ebony shrine. The Dutchman knelt before it.

He spoke softly. "O Master of Darkness," he whispered. "Thank you for delivering these men into my hands. Their arrival is premature, but I promise I will not fail you. Your will is mine. I go forth into death without fear. You will be avenged."

The waiting was over.

Two

His name was Remo and he was bellysmacking. It smarted, diving forty feet from a cliff and landing on his stomach in the reef-shallowed waters of L'Embouchure Bay.

"No, no," Chiun shrieked from the shore, his thin arms waving wildly over a 1920s red and black striped, knee-length bathing costume. "Come back. Come back at once."

Remo sloshed back toward shore in the calf-high water, his abdomen glowing a bright crimson.

Chiun folded his arms across his chest and shook his head, making his beard and the wispy tuft of white hair on his crown dance in the breeze like a banner. "Disgraceful," he said, pointing with a long fingernail to Remo's red belly. "You are soaked. You enter the water like a rock."

20

"Tell that to my stomach. It feels like a ripe tomato that's just been fired out of a cannon. That water's only a foot deep."

"Nine inches more than you need," said the old Oriental, his hazel eyes narrowing into slits above his parchment cheekbones. "The Flying Wall must be performed lightly, like a seagull skimming the waters. The dive was developed in my village of Sinanju in Korea. Perhaps the teachings of Sinanju are too rigorous for soft white men," he said with a tight smile.

"Chiun, I live for Sinanju. But I can't help it. I'm not you. My stomach turns red when I hit a coral reef at a hundred miles an hour. Besides, this is supposed to be our vacation."

"If you are so in need of rest that you cannot perform your exercises, I suggest that you remain abed." He sniffed. "This island sun cannot be good for one's health. Too warm."

Remo's night-dark eyes pinched in sudden understanding. "That's it. You're just ticked 'cause Smitty sent us here for vacation when we could have been lolling on the rocky, frozen shores of Sinanju. Right? Right?"

Chiun shrugged. "What can be expected from a white man? Perhaps Emperor Smith felt you were not sufficiently excellent on our last assignment to merit a stay in Sinanju. Perhaps this desolate, sunfilled place is a fitting punishment for your laziness in performing the exercises recommended by the Master of Sinanju."

"Sint Maarten's one of the most beautiful islands in the world," Remo said stubbornly. "It sure beats the hell out of that back-stabbing rock quarry you call home."

Chiun bristled, the white cloud of hair on his head whipping back and forth. "How dare you insult the name of my village?" he sputtered.

"The last time we set foot in that godforsaken dump, the local clowns tried to murder me," Remo yelled.

"Perhaps they had seen you attempt the Flying Wall. Heh, heh." He pointed to the cliff from which Remo had been diving. "Heh, heh. Flying Wall. More like Flying-Pile-of-Garbage. Heh, heh." He rubbed his stomach in painful reminder.

"Well, they didn't exactly roll out the welcome mat for you, either. After all the gold you've sent them, they all sided with Nuihc, against you. He was calling himself the Master of Sinanju, and they believed him."

Chiun winced with the memory.

The Master of Sinanju was obliged by a thousand-year-old custom to support his village through his earnings as an assassin—the best assassin in history—for the House of Sinanju was the sun source of all the martial arts. Chiun had honored that custom for most of his eighty-odd years. But Nuihc, his nephew, would not. Despite his lofty speeches to the villagers of Sinanju, Nuihc was a greedy, evil man who had lived in dishonor all his life, and planned to sell out the village to the Communist North Koreans as soon as he usurped Chiun's position as Master. Death was too good for him, but death had claimed him anyway.

22

"That is all past now," Chiun said quietly. "Still, my village of Sinanju is lovely in the springtime. Come, Remo. I will show you the Flying Wall."

Remo walked him to the edge of the water and watched as the little man scaled the sheer face of the cliff like a gaily striped spider. He loved the old man who still, in his eighth decade, toiled at the work of death to keep his ungrateful village alive. To Remo, Chiun was Sinanju, and all of the greatness of the training of Sinanju was embodied in him. Remo watched. He wanted to learn the Flying Wall.

The tiny figure on top of the cliff shot off the edge without hesitation. He continued like a projectile almost straight out for some 50 feet before descending. He looked like a colorful bearded bird as he shifted his arms to catch the thermal air pockets in the wind. He descended in a curve toward shore, and landed in the shallowest water without a splash. The momentum of his flight kept him skimming over the corals until he was within inches of Remo. Then he stood up, revealing only a slender band of wetness down the front of his body. Even the backs of his legs were dry.

"That was beautiful, Chiun," Remo said.

The Oriental's eyes sparkled but he said only, "It was adequate to demonstrate the proper shifting of weight." He wrapped himself in a red silk kimono with a dragon embroidered on the back. "I will go back to the house now for dry clothing and a cup of tea," he said.

"Okay. I want to try the Flying Wall a couple of times."

"You will perform the exercise ten times, sloth-ful one," Chiun said.

"Ten? That's the hardest dive I've ever seen. Nobody can do that ten times without getting killed."

"Oh? In that case, we shall meet next in para-dise. Do not fail to breathe during the curved de-scent."

"Ten times," Remo muttered as Chiun padded off toward the villa their employer had rented for them.

It was odd that Smith had sent them to Sint Maarten. Smitty had to be the most tight-fisted man in the United States government. Springing for a villa, complete with private beach and house-keeper, was as alien to Harold W. Smith as eat-ing octopus.

Remo shrugged off the thought as he neared the top of the cliff, his fingertips pulling him in toward the wall of stone as his feet slid smoothly upward. At the top, he cleared his mind of all dis-tractions but the memory of Chiun's powerful dive, and took off. His body, more finely tuned than any athlete's, was on automatic now. He glided out toward the sea on the instincts devel-oped through years of training. His arms moved reflexively, feeling for the air pockets, and wind-milled slowly backward as he began the slow curve downward. The water touched him softly as he saw, inches below him, a school of angel fish swimming between the craggy reefs of coral that would rip a normal diver to shreds. Like a speedboat he skimmed toward shore, emerging nearly dry.

"I did it! I did it!" Remo exulted.

"Nine more times," came a high, squeaky voice from inside the villa.

Remo lay in the sun, his eyes closed, the heat of midday warming his muscles. The ten dives had been exhausting enough, but he had performed the exercise four extra times for good measure. Now all he wanted to do was sleep.

His past came back to him in snatches, as it often did when he was on the brink of sleep. His years in the orphanage, his training as a policeman in Newark, the incredible frame-up that caused his arrest for killing a dope pusher he didn't kill, the sensational kangaroo court trial that touted him as an example of police brutality, his days on Death Row. . . .

It had been a lousy life. And then another frame-up, perpetrated by Harold W. Smith, who had masterminded the whole false arrest mess in the first place: the electric chair didn't work. That made it complete. A fake death for a fake crime. Only nobody knew the death was a fraud except for Harold W. Smith, who pulled his weighty strings from a computer console hidden in the recesses of Folcroft Sanitarium in Rye, New York; another man who conveniently died shortly after Remo's electrocution; and, after several days of unconsciousness, Remo himself.

All very neat. The President of the United

States had wanted a one-man enforcement arm for an illegal organization, CURE, dedicated to fighting crime outside the Constitution, and Smith had delivered Remo: a man with no family ties who was officially dead.

Smitty had chosen Chiun, the Master of the ancient House of Sinanju, to transform Remo from an easy-going cop into a smooth, perfect killing machine. All the pieces fit into place. There was little room for error, because error would mean the instantaneous destruction of CURE. If Smith failed to keep CURE secret, his death was sealed in a vial of poison in the basement of Folcroft. If Remo failed, Chiun was instructed to kill him at the moment of Smith's order. If the President failed, he was to pass along the information about CURE's existence to his successor in the White House.

Remo hadn't liked it. He didn't want to train with the irascible old Oriental in the beginning, didn't like the cloak-and-dagger secrecy of Smith and CURE, and he certainly didn't like killing people for a living. America went on, after all, even if there was a lot of crime that went unpunished, even if the Constitution, written for decent men, was manipulated inside out by criminals who preyed on decent men under its full protection. Remo could see no need for CURE.

Then the President of the United States was murdered in cold blood by an assassin's bullet. The man who had conceived of CURE as a last-ditch effort to bring crime under control was himself destroyed by crime, and that was when Remo first understood the importance of CURE.

Remo felt a shadow pass in front of his closed eyelids. He opened them slowly to a vision of two bountiful breasts scantily encased by a purple bikini top.

"You are going to burn here," the owner of the breasts said in a lilting accent.

"What?"

She pressed a spot on his forearm. When she released the pressure, the spot emerged white in a field of hot pink. "The sun," she said, pointing upward. "You will burn the skin. You must go inside, or the sunburn will be very bad."

Remo squinted to get a better look at the girl. She was beautiful, with long auburn hair streaming carelessly from a knot on the top of her head. She had bottle-green eyes that danced mischievously under long black lashes. Her mouth was full and ripe, and she was very tan.

"No bathing suit marks," Remo said flirtatiously. Chiun was a great teacher, but as an after-dinner companion, he was a bust. "You look like an experienced tourist."

"I live here," the girl said. She extended her hand. "My name is Fabienne de la Soubise."

"Remo Williams," he said.

"You are American?"

Remo nodded.

"I am French, but here on the island we are all Sint Maarteners. Welcome." She smiled and gave his hand a squeeze. She started to pull away, but Remo got to his feet before she could let go of him. "Say, as long as we've got so much in common, how about us seeing each other again?"

She took in Remo's body with a discreet glance: the thin lines of his frame, his dancer's legs, the well-shaped meat of his shoulders, the thick wrists. His face was handsome in a masculine way, with its deep-set brown eyes and heavy, straight brows, its high cheekbones and firm mouth and clean jaw. A man's man, to be sure. But a woman's man in bed. "Of course," she said. "Can you come to my house tonight?"

"Tonight? Sure—"

A clatter of pots and pans clanking angrily directed his attention toward the kitchen of the villa, where a fat black woman wearing a red bandana on her head emerged banging a soup pan with a wooden spoon.

"You!" she bellowed, waddling toward them with determination in every step. "I thought you already inside," she said crankily, shaking her head in dismay. "You been out here for more than five hour. You gonna fry. All you white men de same—"

"Hello, Sidonie," the girl said with a smile.

"Fabienne!" She slapped Remo's arm with the spoon. "What you doing talking to a nice island girl like her? Gonna give her fancy mainland ideas, make her leave us." She waddled up to Fabienne and kissed her wetly and noisily on the cheek.

"I've just met Remo. He seems a perfect gentleman."

The housekeeper eyed Remo with a twinkle.

28

"He all right for a white man," she said. Remo pinched her ample hindquarter, and she hit him with the spoon again.

"Hey, if you're going to be running my life for the next two weeks, I demand a cease-fire," Remo said.

"I like to run your life, child. Get you to eat some decent food." She turned to Fabienne and said something that sounded to Remo like "Hee Ho Hee Hee Da Bo Wa Wee Tee No Mee Ha."

Fabienne clucked sympathetically and responded, "Hey He Hah Key Hee Hoo Die Ho Hee Noo."

"Beg pardon?" Remo asked.

"Sidonie says you eat nothing but brown rice and tea."

Remo shuffled half apologetically in the sand. "I don't know. I eat other things. Duck, sometimes. A little fish—"

"Raw he eats it," Sidonie said with disgust. "These fanatical Americans, always with the health food."

Fabienne took Remo's hand again. "And I told her that I cook very good brown rice. I like raw fish, too."

"You do?"

"Come see me tonight. My driver will be here at seven, but take as long as you like," she said.

"I'll be ready at seven." Remo beamed as the girl waved to them both and walked away with the purposeful, athletic stride of a rich girl weaned on tennis and horseback riding.

"Now you go inside," Sidonie said. "The old

gentleman, he already in his room, looking at the TV. I got your lunch."

She took Remo to a big wooden table in the kitchen, set before him a bowl of brown rice and a cup of green tea, and poured herself a big tumbler of dark rum as she settled her bulky body on a chair beside him.

"Not bad," Remo said, tasting the rice. Sidonie grunted. "Say, what language were you speaking back there with Fabienne?"

"That Papiamento. The native tongue."

"I thought the native tongue was English."

"Oh, we all speak English. Also French and Dutch, some Spanish. This island so mixed up with all the Europeans come to steal her away from us, they teach us all their languages. So we put them together in Papiamento. It easier—also the white man don't understand."

"The girl's white."

"She different. She be here all her life. Her daddy a fine man, too." She shook her head sadly. "Dead now."

"Recently?" Remo asked.

"Couple of year. First he go cuckoo, then he dead." She polished off the contents of her glass and refilled it with the same fumey liquid. "I work for Monsieur Soubise for many year. During the war, he take me back to Paris with him." She grinned broadly. "Monsieur and Sidonie, we fight for the Resistance."

"Is that where you learned to drink like a sailor?" Remo asked wryly.

Sidonie tapped the rim of her glass. "This pure

island rum. Good for the digestion." She hic-cupped. "Also it give a good buzz."

With some difficulty Sidonie lifted herself off her chair and waddled around the kitchen, straightening containers and dusting the window-sills. "Anyway, Fabienne, she's a good girl. Always have something nice to say, even now that she lose all her money."

"That's funny," Remo said. "She seemed like a rich girl."

"Oh, her daddy very, very rich. But he go cuck-oo." In demonstration she twirled a corkscrew in the air beside her temple. "He change his will, leave everything—the shipyards, everything—to the Dutchman. And Monsieur, he don't even know the Dutchman. Cuckoo."

"Who's the Dutchman?" Remo asked.

Sidonie's eyes narrowed. "He no good," she said. "Live on Devil's Mountain in the old castle. He cuckoo, too."

Remo laughed. "I guess the old monsieur was happy to find a kindred spirit."

"Don't you talk about the Dutchman with Fa-bienne. It just upset her. He take all her money, and she fighting two year in the court now trying to get it back. She very upset, poor thing."

"She can't be that poor," Remo said consolingly. "She's got a driver."

Sidonie snorted. "Dat just Pierre," she said. "He don't cost much. Pierre do anything for a dollah. Don't you talk to him neither. This island, she nosy. And Pierre got a big mouth on him."

"Okay, okay," Remo said.

31

"You listen to Sidonie, child, you be all right here." She chuckled and squeezed his cheek between fat brown fingers.

The footsteps banged forward like a fleet of Sherman tanks. How was a being of delicate sensibilities, whose only pleasure in the twilight of his years was the viewing of the pure love stories presented on the touching daytime dramas, supposed to concentrate on the vicissitudes of life with the clamor of 10,000 giants outside his window?

Chiun leaped up and switched off the Betamax, which was airing a 1965 episode of "As the Planet Revolves." "Out," he shouted to the world at large. "Leave my presence immediately, noisy lout, or . . ."

Two weary eyes beneath a twenty-year-old straw fedora peered at him over the windowsill.

"Emperor Smith," Chiun said, suddenly bowing obsequiously to the man who sent the yearly tribute of gold via submarine to Chiun's village. "My heart thrills with this honor." His hazel eyes darted back for a longing moment to the blank TV screen. "As the Planet Revolves" was infinitely more interesting than Harold W. Smith, even during the commercials.

"Can I—can I come in?" Smith said with utter solemnity as his head, framed by the open window, craned suspiciously in all directions.

"At your service, o esteemed Emperor," Chiun said, groaning inwardly. Smith's careworn, withered lemon face had "meeting" stamped all over it. The blank eye of the Betamax stared mockingly. Chiun extended a hand to Smith, who was trying to crawl through the window, his face contorted in agony as he sought a toehold with the tips of his Florsheims. With a light flick of the Oriental's wrist, Smith sailed over the Betamax and came to rest on a plump cushion in the corner.

With a smile and a bow, Chiun began to wheel the television toward the door. "One moment, most worthy Emperor, and I will command Remo to your presence here—"

"No," Smith whispered urgently. He rose from his sprawled position on the cushion, reassuming his habitual air of bland dignity. "Remo is in the kitchen talking to the housekeeper. That's why I came this way instead of to the door. I have to speak with you alone."

Chiun's eyes brightened. "I see, o magnificence," he said conspiratorially. "A private mission . . . an assignment for another government perhaps?" He winked.

"Chiun," Smith said, flustered, "we work for the United States."

"Governments come and depart in the night. But an assassin is a treasure forever. Yet I will do as you bid, Emperor. . . ."

"Good. I was counting on that. . . ."

"As soon as we arrive at a mutually comfortable and honorable fee for my duties. Perhaps twenty thousand in gold. . . ."

"This is part of our original contract, Chiun."

"Oh." The old Oriental's eyes wandered back to the blank Betamax.

Smith nervously rolled his hat in his hands. "Let

me explain as quickly as I can, before Remo happens along."

"By all means," Chiun said, stifling a yawn.

"You've probably been wondering why I sent the two of you to Sint Maarten for your vacation."

"Not at all," Chiun said, feigning disinterest. "If you in your wisdom did not see fit to grant an old man his only wish of seeing his village of Sinanju . . ." He closed his eyes and shrugged expressively.

"I was planning to, but something came up." From inside his coat pocket he extracted a large envelope containing a dozen or more photographs. He leafed through the pictures and handed one to Chiun. It showed a large ship with a crane on its deck hoisting a long rectangular metal box out of the ocean. "A U.S. salvage ship dredged up this truck body nearby, off the coast of the island."

"Ah, most fascinating," Chiun said. "Have you by any chance been privileged to observe the beautiful daytime dramas on the television?" He scurried over to the Betamax. "Perhaps, if we are fortunate, Dr. Rad Rex will appear in 'As the Planet Revolves.'"

"Chiun—really—"

Smith was too late. Chiun had already pushed the magic switch that brought Dr. Rad Rex and the suffering Mrs. Wintersheim back into the room just as Mrs. Wintersheim was revealing her guilty secret involving her daughter's marriage to Carl Aberdeen's podiatrist, Skip. The old man was settled in front of the television, smiling raptly, his

34

lips mouthing the words he had heard thousands of times before.

Brushing a hand over his eyes, Smith knelt beside him. "Chiun, the sunken truck container in that photo I just showed you contained more than a hundred dead bodies of unidentifiable men."

"Tsk, tsk," Chiun conceded.

"The point is, someone murdered them."

"Here today, gone tomorrow," Chiun murmured.

Smith squeezed his eyes shut. Briskly he took out another photograph. "I think Remo killed them," he said.

Chiun nodded. "Perhaps they offended him."

"Will you please look at these?" Smith asked, thrusting the sheaf of photographs in front of Chiun.

With a sigh, the old man turned first his head, then his eyes in the direction of the pictures. Then slowly his hand reached out and depressed the "Off" button on the Betamax. "Remarkable," he said.

"I thought you'd recognize the style."

"These attacks were nearly perfect," he said beaming. "Oh, a little sloppy with this third vertebra, slow inside line here—details, details. Overall, this is most excellent work. I congratulate you, o Emperor."

"On what?"

"On your most astute perception of my pupil's progress. Will you give him a medal?" Chiun nodded expectantly.

Smith cleared his throat. "That's not exactly what I had in mind."

"Oh!" Chiun slapped his forehead. "Of course. You are a man of great wisdom, Emperor Smith. Many thanks, o illustrious one. I shall display it with great pride and humility."

"Display what?"

"My medal, of course. Only one of truly keen acumen such as yourself would seek to reward the student by honoring the teacher. I am deeply touched by this tribute."

"Chiun, you don't understand. I've never assigned Remo to these islands before."

"So? An assassin with skill such as I have taught Remo can kill here as well as anywhere."

"I was afraid of that," Smith said. His face was drawn and haggard. "Please listen to me, Chiun. I haven't got much time, and I have to explain something to you. If Remo didn't kill those men in the truck on assignment, that means he's been killing them on his own. You know I can't permit that. It was part of our initial deal."

Chiun's smile faded as Smith's meaning became clear. "Perhaps he was only practicing?" Chiun offered.

"It doesn't matter what the reason was. If Remo has gone off on a killing spree, he must be stopped."

"Yes," Chiun said softly. "It was our agreement."

"And you must stop him."

The old man slowly nodded assent.

"It should be done at an appropriate time, and

36

with no witnesses. That's why I rented the villa for you. You'll have to dispose of the—uh—"

Chiun held up a hand for silence. After a moment, Smith stood up awkwardly beside the frail old teacher who sat with his back bent and his head bowed.

"This is the end for all of us," Smith whispered, his voice cracking. "After you report back to me at Folcroft, you'll be sent back to Sinanju, and . . ." There was no need to explain that Remo's death would mean the end of CURE, since Chiun had never known who his employer was beyond Harold W. Smith. And there was no need to point out that Smith's own life would end with Remo's, in the basement of Folcroft Sanitarium. There was, in fact, no need to say anything more. Quietly, Smith walked back to the window. As he removed his hat in preparation for his exit, Remo walked into the room.

"Smitty," he said. "What are you doing here?"

"Uh—vacationing. With Mrs. Smith. On Saba, uh, nearby island." Smith had never been a good liar. He nodded tersely and strode toward the door.

"Hey, wait a minute. You two look like senior projects at undertakers' school. What's going on?"

Smith shook his head, cleared his throat again, and said, "Good day," without looking at either of the men in the room. Chiun sat motionless, his head bowed. "Oh, I nearly forgot," Smith said. He took a parchment-colored envelope from his breast pocket and slid it on the floor beside Chiun. "It was on your doorstep, but I saw the wind blow it into the bushes. Thought I'd better hand it to you myself before it got lost." He touched his fingers to his hat and was gone.

"What in the hell has happened to Smitty?" Remo said, laughing. "First he puts us here in deluxe accommodations, then he comes here on vacation. That old skinflint hasn't taken a vacation in fifteen years, and the last time was to visit his wife's uncle in Idaho. . . ."

Chiun wasn't listening. His breath was catching as his hand moved slowly toward the envelope beside him.

"What is it?" Remo asked. "You feeling all right, Little Father?"

Chiun snatched up the envelope and held it with both hands up to the light. On it in both English and Korean, was written the name "CHIUN" with thick black brush strokes. In a frenzy the old man tore open the envelope and yanked out a single translucent piece of old, dried rice paper.

Then Chiun did something so strange, so unlike himself, so terrifying, that Remo couldn't believe his eyes. The old man leaped up from the floor, bounded toward Remo, encircled him in his frail, bony arms, and held him.

"Wha-what?" Remo stammered. "Little Father, are you okay?" Chiun said nothing, but held fast. "I mean the dives were pretty good, if I do say so myself, but . . . C'mon, I'm not used to this. Hey, it's the envelope, isn't it, Chiun? What'd you get? A fan letter from Sinanju. That's it, isn't it, a fan letter?"

Still caught in the old man's embrace, he turned

to see the piece of paper in Chiun's hand. On it were three carefully drawn Korean characters.

"What's it say, Chiun?" Remo asked.

Chiun broke away. "It says 'I live again.' "

Remo half smiled, trying to share Chiun's joy. "I live again? That's it, huh?"

"That is the message. 'I live again.' "

"Hey . . . great. Good news. Really glad to hear it. Who lives again?"

"Never mind," Chiun said. He tucked the paper into a fold of his kimono sleeve.

"Well, whoever it was, I'm glad he gave you such a lift. Say, I've been thinking maybe we could take a little sightseeing tour of the island before dark—"

"You will perform ten more Flying Walls," Chiun snapped.

"What? I just did fourteen!"

"Fourteen of the most slovenly examples of the Flying Wall I have ever had the misfortune to witness. Your descent was at least a handspan too steep."

"It was not. You weren't even watching. . . ."

"Ten," Chiun decreed.

Glaring over his shoulder, Remo shuffled toward the door. "See if I ever ask you again. . . ."

"Ten."

After the door closed, the old man smiled.

Three

There were six women in the room, two blondes, three brunettes, and an Asian. They were all naked, their smooth flanks glistening in the dim colored light of the room as they lounged unceremoniously along the heavy padding of the floor.

There were no courtesan's squeals to greet the Dutchman as he entered; he was only annoyed by such preliminaries. He took the one nearest to him, a blonde, and directed her languid hand to his body. Her jaw was slack. As she brought him mechanically to readiness, he saw the pinpoint pupils of her eyes beneath the heavy, sodden lids.

Roughly he pulled her left arm up toward the light to confirm the inevitable appearance of the track marks on the bruised skin. An addict. She would be sent away tomorrow. He did not tolerate drug usage among the women he hired. It emptied their minds. They could be of no use to him beyond providing receptacles for his passion.

He pushed her aside. The girl slumped to the floor where she had stood. The Dutchman grabbed the hair of the next girl and forced her head back, pulling up the skin of her eyelids to check for the same symptoms. When he was convinced she was in normal health, he eased her to the floor. Silently she submitted to him while the others in the room sat back, their expressions bored, as each waited her turn.

He went through four of them, each shattering climax fueling his terrible energy more than the last until his pale skin shone with sweat and his nerves were as sensitive as live electric wires.

The Asiatic took his thrusts with stoic docility, her almond eyes veiled and impersonal.

"You are a tigress," he said to her in French, her language. He wanted no one in the Castle who spoke English, to better guard his privacy. The Dutchman himself spoke eight languages, plus the arcane sign language he used with his mute servant, so there was no privacy from the Dutchman.

The girl's quiet eyes suddenly burned with bright fire. "You are an animal of the jungle," the Dutchman whispered. "Your claws are sharp. Your teeth shine with the promise of death." With an effort, he restrained the girl from raking his back with her long, blood-red fingernails. She bared her teeth in a cat's grimace. Something deep in her throat growled with feline pleasure.

He fought her, there on the padded white floor,

as her knee-length black hair whipped around them both in frenetic passion. Her curled hand struck at his face. He slammed it to the floor above her head and rode her until she screamed in defeat and satiation.

He was ablaze. He was ready now. Naked and slick with sweat, he left the girl panting on the floor with the others and walked into a small courtyard lined on one end with straw dummies. In the open end of the yard, he performed the difficult exercises he had begun when he was a child. He was twenty-four years old now. He had been slowly mastering the exercises for fourteen years.

The Dutchman came out of a sustained three-finger stand and vaulted in two triple flying somersaults to the straw figures standing like sentries. With a stroke of his hand, he lopped off the head of one of the dummies, which had been affixed to its body by a four-by-four-inch post. He removed the arms with thrusts of each elbow, the thick wooden supports cracking and splitting with each lightning-fast jab.

He took on the dummies as he had the women, swiftly, methodically, emotionless. When he had finished, the courtyard was strewn with straw and sawdust and splinters of wood. The Dutchman was at peak now, his muscles prepared, his mind ranging like a predator around the isolated yard.

He had never learned to control the wild, awesome thing inside his brain that sought release only through destruction. Perhaps it was impossible to control. There had only been a few cases like it throughout all of human history, and those rare specimens had spent their lives in confinement, under the fearful scrutiny of scientists. They had lived like rats in a laboratory cage.

The Master had seen to it that Jeremiah had not shared their fate. Instead, he had prepared the boy's body to become as lethal as his mind. Together, the combination was to have helped the Master gain the world.

But death had claimed the Master before the boy came of age, and his murder had gone unavenged. During that time the Dutchman trained and practiced and waited for his twenty-fifth year—the year when, according to the Master, Jeremiah would be ready to undertake the responsibilities of his destiny and come a man into his Master's world.

"There are only two others on the earth who can match me," the Dutchman roared into the silence of the courtyard. "Two who can match me in strength and skill. And even though I face them before my time, they will be dead before the week is out because they do not possess my mind!" In a rage, he lifted up one of the blocks of wood that had fallen from the straw dummies and hurled it high into the air, over the courtyard wall, beyond the castle grounds, and out of sight.

"Chiun!" his voice echoed savagely off the stone courtyard walls. "Remo! You have stumbled into my domain to meet your end."

He was pulled out of the insensate roarings of his mind by the close yapping of a small animal. Already out of control, he turned slowly to see with his madman's eyes a dog darting back and

43

forth in the courtyard, barking bravely at the Dutchman whom all animals feared.

His eyes automatically trained themselves on the dog. With a yelp, the animal began to run faster and faster around the courtyard, panting, stumbling over its own feet, until it collapsed. Its tongue lolled out in exhaustion.

The Dutchman tried to pull his mind away from the dog. It belonged to the Asiatic girl, and she was his favorite. But he could no more quell the violent power of his thoughts than he could halt the tide. He felt the thing, the ugly, unwanted thing inside him that had given him no rest since the moment he had discovered it, stir within him. The dog would have to die another horrifying death to add to the Dutchman's long list.

The thought was emerging on its own, red and blistery, the colors growing brighter. . . . Then the sound of fast, shuffling feet momentarily broke his concentration as the girl, clothed in a white sleeping gown, her black hair flying behind her, dashed into the courtyard and scooped the dog up in her arms. She was whimpering and her hands shook as she picked up the animal, careful not to look at the Dutchman.

But the thought had already formed. *Boils*. And suddenly the girl screamed and tore at her clothes in a grotesque frenzy. The white gown hung in tattered strands over her once-perfect body, now covered with seeping sores. The dog scurried into the interior of the castle as the girl clawed at her eyes. Her ragged cries echoed, feeding the Killing Picture in the Dutchman's wild, transfixed eyes.

It was near the end. The girl's knees buckled and she fell to the earth, still screaming. Then the doorway opened, and the mute stood within its arch, the little dog at his feet.

"No!" the Dutchman shouted, but the mute would not leave. When would it stop, the horror, the killing, the revulsion at himself? Would he spend the rest of his life killing everyone who dared to come near him? Would he end his days a senseless monster with no will to perform anything but acts of death? With an effort so great that he felt his heart would stop, the Dutchman's feet began to turn. One step, then another, each harder than the last, until he was facing the wall.

"Go," he whispered hoarsely. The mute ran into the courtyard and lifted the bleeding girl in his arms. Then they fled with the little dog whining beside them through the big oak and iron door leading inside the castle.

The Dutchman clung to the top of the wall with white-knuckled hands. He could not hang on much longer. Soon he would have to turn back, commanded by the demon inside him, and everything in his way would be obliterated.

When he heard the soft thump of the door closing, the tension lessened. He felt some strength return to his hands and legs. Jumping high into the air, he vaulted over the wall and ran over the scrub of Devil's Mountain to the sea, where he swam for several miles until his energy began to dissipate.

Far out in the deep waters of the Atlantic, the demon calmed. The Dutchman turned on his back to see the bright, clean streaks of sunset clouds in the sky. His nostrils filled with the salt fragrance of the sea. His body floated motionless on the waves, soothed and cooled by the water. It would be so easy here, now, to dive to the depths of the sea, attach himself to a rock, and release the life from him that would float to the surface with the air in his lungs and burst in the salt spray. Death would be the most welcome event in his life.

But death was a luxury he could not give himself before his task was completed. He had made a promise to the Master, and he would fulfill it. Remo and Chiun would die first. Then the Dutchman would rest.

With long, weary strokes, he swam back to shore.

The mute was waiting for him when he returned to the castle. With his usual stony expression, he prepared the Dutchman his bath and a solitary meal of rice and tea. After he had finished, the Dutchman said, "Thank you, Sanchez." It was the first time he had used the mute's name. Sanchez's expression did not change, but the Dutchman thought he saw, for a brief moment, something like pity flicker in the mute's eyes.

The Dutchman spoke no more. In sign language, he asked Sanchez to make preparations at the shipyard. He could not allow more incidents to occur in his own home. The straw dummies were not adequate to contain his strength. He needed live victims.

The mute nodded and left. *My power is becom-*

ing frightening, the Dutchman thought. *Soon I will have to make contact with the young American and the old Oriental, Chiun. The time is coming.*

Soon.

Four

Pierre came to get Remo in a red Datsun pickup. Its fenders were riddled with dents, and the tailgate clanked open and shut with each bump on the winding dirt roads. Both headlights were smashed.

"Is this thing safe?" Remo asked.

"Safest car on de road," Pierre said, his teeth shining brilliant white against the ebony blackness of his skin. He patted the pitted dashboard of the Datsun as it labored up the steep hill roads near the island's west shore. "When Pierre get in accident, he drive away. Other guy—splat." He grinned with homicidal glee.

"Isn't that illegal?" Remo asked, amused.

Pierre dismissed the objection. "Not much illegal in the islands," he said. "Killing with gun, that illegal. Squashing with car, that legal." He poked

Remo in the ribs. "Good thing for you Pierre got big car, huh?"

Remo smiled wanly. On his right, far below the cliff road, he spotted an industrial complex surrounded by an electric fence replete with high-voltage signs in English, French, and Dutch. Two television monitors atop high metal poles tracked the area constantly. The entire place was lit with bright floodlights.

The elaborate security system made the compound seem out of place in its primitive, night-blackened setting. "What's that?" Remo asked, pointing to it.

"Dat the Soubise shipyards," Pierre said.

"Soubise? Fabienne's father?"

"Dat the one. Only Soubise, he dead now. It all belong to the Dutchman now." He whispered the name in a low, mysterious whisper designed more for intrigue than communication.

"That Dutchman again. Everybody keeps bringing up the Dutchman, like he's some kind of a ghost. Who is this guy, anyway?"

"Nobody know the Dutchman," Pierre said, his voice that of a master storyteller beginning to spin his tale. "Never see nobody, never go noplace, that one. Some say he the devil himself. Look. Look up there." He skidded the truck to a halt on the steep mountain road, causing the vehicle to shimmy precariously close to the cliff.

"What's that?" Remo said, squinting through the darkness at a barbaric-looking white fortress on a hill in the distance.

49

"Dat the castle where he live, the Dutchman, up on Devil's Mountain."

"A castle? Must be an eccentric old coot."

"He just a boy, Mister Remo," Pierre whispered. "Maybe twenty, twenty-five year old. But he the devil, don't doubt that."

Remo was interested. "Sidonie said Old Man Soubise left him all his money."

"And the shipyard, too. The old man, he see the Dutchman, and he go cuckoo. Dat what happen. Any man what looks on the golden boy of the castle, it too late." His eyes rolled in a broad pantomime of instantaneous madness.

"Wait a minute, Pierre. That kind of stuff's pure superstition."

"It true!" Pierre protested. "The Dutchman, he go in disguise to work for Monsieur Soubise as a truck loader. One day he get close to the old man, and bam! Like that, the old man say he a bird and jump off a cliff."

"Which cliff?"

"Dis one."

Remo checked again out the window, where the truck teetered near the edge. "Speaking of the cliff, Pierre—"

"My cousin, he seen it happen," Pierre said stubbornly. "It turn out the old man change his will that day, just before he fly off the cliff saying he's a bird, and he leave everything to the Dutchman. Then, when the Dutchman take over, he put up the electric fence and the TV cameras." With that, the rear of the stopped truck settled noisily into the soft shoulder of the cliff.

"How are we going to get this tank moving again at this angle?" Remo asked irritably.

Pierre smiled. "No problem, boss." After a scream of grinding gears, he yanked the truck into reverse and whistled cheerfully as they careened backward down the darkened, one-lane road.

"Watch it!" Remo yelled. "You don't have any lights. What if somebody's coming the other way?"

"Oh, don't worry, Mister Remo. This here's big truck. Anybody come in our way, we cream 'em."

Remo shut his eyes and waited for the inevitable crash. It figured, he thought. More than a decade of the finest physical training on earth, and he was going to be killed at the hands of a lunatic island truck driver.

After a few minutes of Pierre's reverse roller coaster ride down the mountain, the truck drifted to a halt.

" 'S'okay, boss," Pierre said with confidence.

Remo opened his eyes cautiously. Pierre was holding a flashlight to the window. "We back at the bottom. Now we just go up again."

Before the truck stretched two roads. One was the treacherous, winding climb up the mountain they had just descended with such hellish speed. The other was a straight, gravel-paved, two-lane road leading up the same hill. Pierre switched off the flashlight decisively and punched the truck into gear to begin the tortuous climb up the first road.

"Wait a second," Remo said. "The other road looked a lot better. Why don't we go that way?"

The islander shook his head elaborately. "Nuh-huh. No way, *suh*."

"Why not? Don't these roads intersect?"

"Yes," Pierre agreed amiably, bouncing in his seat from the rutted potholes in the road.

"Then why don't we use the other one, for crying out loud?"

"Dat road lead to Devil's Mountain. Ain't using it."

"This is nut-house time," Remo said, exasperated. "You're telling me you won't even drive a truck on a better road just because it happens to lead to the place where this weirdo Dutchman lives?"

"Yup," Pierre said, snapping his jaw shut.

There would be no more discussion of the route after that, Remo knew. He had seen Chiun use the same final gesture often enough. He sat back, accustoming himself to the ordeal of the long drive up the hill, when he heard a sound like the buzzing of insects. "What's that?" he asked.

"Motorcycle. Dirt bike, maybe. People's got 'em up here, where folks got money."

"I don't see any lights."

Pierre shrugged. "Who need lights?"

Remo sighed. Then the buzzing grew louder, came up beside the truck, and flew ahead.

"Funny," Pierre said. "I still don't see nothing."

Remo peered into the darkness. "It's funny, all right." In front of them, the dirt bike slowed down to stay just ahead of the truck. The driver was clad all in black, hiding him in the night. As Remo watched, a black face turned around, and an arm came up holding a pistol.

"Get down," Remo yelled, pulling Pierre down into his seat as the biker squeezed off two shots into the truck's cabin and took off.

The bullets left two round o's encased in spider-webbed glass on the passenger side of the windshield.

"You fast, boss," Pierre said, wiping the sweat off his forehead. "Plenty fast."

"Got any enemies?" Remo asked.

"I don't know." Pierre smiled. "Guess so, huh?"

Fabienne's sprawling island ranch house stood nearby in Bilboquet, the Beverly Hills of Sint Maarten. The homes in the area belonged mostly to wealthy foreigners who lived in them a few weeks out of each year, leaving them fully staffed but vacant the rest of the time. Few of the residents were permanent—the founder of the Sint Maarten Bank of Commerce, Mr. Potts, the rum king, whose distilleries dotted the coast, an East Indian merchant-prince whose chain of boutiques catered to tourists looking for "genuine" island fashions, a Japanese importer of Sony electronics and Seiko watches, and a nineteen-year-old American millionaire with a penchant for disco music who, it was reputed, had made his fortune smuggling one single shipment of cocaine into the United States. All in all, the motley group "on the hill," as the natives referred to Bilboquet, were not particularly fascinating to Fabienne de la Soubise.

Her father, Henri, had built the house on the hill only when his wife had deemed intolerable the old stone mansion near the shipyard, where his family had lived for four generations. The three acres on Bilboquet separated them from their jet-setting neighbors, but not enough for Henri or his offspring Fabienne, who had inherited his temperament as well as his features. Fabienne had grown up loving the island and the big ships full of blustering, rough-talking seamen with whom her father did business. When the first surge of tourism came, her mother reveled in their new-found social life with its glittering parties and expensive European shops. Of course, her mother would explain, those were the *real* people, the wealthy nobs who sailed their party yachts to the island for a stay of a month or more, not to be confused with the late-coming honeymooners and week vacationers who arrived via package flights to stay at the newly built Holiday Inns. Fabienne didn't care. She liked the islanders much more than the tourists—real or otherwise—and had learned their tongue early from her father.

When her mother left them both to fly back to Paris, her father had taken her desertion hard. He spent interminable hours at the shipyard office, building an even greater fortune than he had inherited, which was reflected in the magnificent furnishings of the house in Bilboquet, although he rarely saw it: Louix XV dining chairs; twin waist-high Ming Dynasty vases of translucent green; an enormous eight-by-four-foot table carved from a single California redwood, shipped from America;

a silk divan from Napoleon's sitting room at Fontainbleau, restuffed with eiderdown. He had wanted Fabienne's life to be as luxurious and patrician as his own was lonely and overworked.

Thank God for the furniture. Selling it had kept her alive, she thought as she strung a small gold loop through her ear. They were the last earrings she had left. Henri would roll over in his grave if he saw the state in which he had left his only child after his inexplicable bout with lunacy, which ended his own life and gave everything his family had worked for 200 years to a strange young man no one on the island had ever known except by the most outlandish rumors. She had sued the occupant of the Castle, whatever his name was, for a return of her legacy, but even at best, legal proceedings moved with elephantine slowness on the island, never mind when no one could be found who was willing to serve court papers on the man. She had tried herself, but was effectively driven away each time by his servant, a small, menacing-looking man with an arsenal of hand-to-hand weapons strung in his belt and whose only sounds were the eerie moans of someone who'd suffered irreparable damage to his voice mechanism. She would try again. There was nothing else to do.

The bell rang, and a smile spread across her face as she walked through the rambling house to the front door, once answered only by servants. These were bad times, she knew, but there were bright spots even now. Like the young man behind the door.

Remo smiled almost shyly as she took his hand and led him past the vestibule into the living room. His smile turned to surprise as he looked around. She laughed; she had become used to the small embarrassments of her rare guests.

"I didn't say I could entertain you in style," she said as she led him to one of the two cushions in the room, the only furniture apart from a brace of candles on a ceramic dish on the floor.

"I know you won't believe it, but this is exactly the style I'm used to," Remo said.

She laughed, a big, hearty, uninhibited guffaw. "That's the nicest thing you could have said." Her green eyes caught the sparkle of the candles. She took his hand. "I've chilled some champagne," she said. "Found it in the cellar."

Remo placed his hand on her hair, found a pin, and removed it. The cascade tumbled over her shoulders, nestling between her breasts. Remo pulled her close to him and kissed her. She responded eagerly, holding him as her lips parted to feel the smooth pressure of his tongue.

"I don't feel like drinking," Remo said.

She kissed him again. "Maybe we can think of another activity."

She responded to Remo's tender, expert lovemaking with the zeal of a woman who'd sworn off sex for years, only to rediscover it with more joy than she had ever felt. When they were finished, they held each other in a riot of tangled, damp sheets on Fabienne's bed, the only piece of furniture left in the room.

Remo stroked her face, now shiny and content-edly drowsy. "I'm glad we're here together," he said.

She nuzzled her face close to his chest. "Monsieur Remo Williams," she said very close to him, "you are possibly the best lover in the world."

"Possibly?" Remo snorted in mock indignation. "Not positively?"

"Positively, this has been the most wonderful hour I've spent in—in many years." Her face flickered and darkened for a moment with unwanted memories.

"At least two years," Remo said.

"How did you . . ." She waved the rest of her question away. People talked, especially on the island. "I guess you didn't believe I just like empty houses, did you?"

"I'm sorry. Is there anything I can do?"

She shook her head. "Nothing, I'm afraid. It's up to the courts now. Don't bother about my financial ups and downs, Remo. We only have a short time together. Let us enjoy what we can, *quoi*?" She cocked her head beguilingly. In the moonlight she looked, Remo thought, like a good French postcard.

"*Saisez le jour*'s what I always say." He pulled her face to his.

She looked bewildered. "I beg your pardon?"

"*Saisez le—*" He cleared his throat. "It's French. I think. Catch the day. Grab the moment. Or maybe it means pass the salt. I never was very good in high school French."

57

"Oh." She burst into peals of laughter. "*Chéri*, your French is wonderful." She kissed him. "Where it matters."

She climbed out of bed and reached for Remo's hand. "Come with me," she said. "I want to show you something."

She led him outside, where the warm trade winds were singing through the silhouettes of the palm trees. "It's beautiful," Remo said, because he knew she wanted him to say it.

"It gets better."

They walked behind the house, through a bright tropical garden that Fabienne had maintained, past a grove of mango trees, until the sound of slapping water came up at them from whitecaps far below. "This is the best spot on the island," Fabienne said, testing a rock with her foot. The rock gave way and tumbled down the cliff to splash in the sea. "One just has to be careful where one sits." She sat down cross-legged near the cliff, her naked limbs shimmering.

Remo sat next to her, his arm encircling her shoulders. "One promises to be very careful," he said. "One would not like to slide down this cliff without so much as one's pair of jockey shorts to smooth one's way."

She laughed. "You're making fun of my accent."

"I'm crazy about your accent. Among other things."

She started to speak, but Remo silenced her. There was something else in the air, a familiar noise.

"Are there any motorcycle trails around here?"

58

"I suppose," she said. "Not in my back yard, surely. Remo . . ."

But the sound grew more persistent. "Someone took a potshot at Pierre's truck tonight," he said. "Someone on a dirt bike."

By then, the presence of the bike was undeniable. "Get behind those trees," Remo said.

"What will you do?"

"I'm going to get a better look at him. Go on." He pushed her near the grove of fruit trees that dominated the skyline. Remo walked along the cliff, toward the source of the motorcycle's blast.

He could see it now, headed straight for him. As the bike approached, a blinding beam from its headlamp focused on Remo. He held up his arms, waving. "Get out of here," he shouted. "This is private property." But the bike kept speeding for him, accelerating as it came closer. When he realized that the biker wasn't going to stop, he sidestepped out of the way as the bike veered dangerously close. Maybe the bullets weren't for Pierre, Remo mused. But who in this place would want . . .

Fabienne's scream echoed in the still night as the dirt bike entered the grove of mango trees. The rider had found the girl. Remo raced back while the bike's engine roared in short bursts as it raced around the maze of the grove. He saw Fabienne running out of the trees, followed by the bike a few feet behind. A silhouetted arm on the bike's handlebars raised slowly, a pistol poised at the end of it aiming for the girl.

Automatically Remo squeezed his eyes shut to

help his night vision. Then he picked up a small rock at his feet and hurled it. The rock was smaller than a baseball, but it shattered the gun to fragments in the man's hand. It gave Remo enough time to reach the girl and toss her gently to the ground, out of the way.

The bike came at them again, circling and buzzing menacingly. Remo waited for it to come near enough to pull the driver off. But even as it drew close and he got a clear picture of the driver's bloated, outlaw's face, the figure in black drew something from his pocket. It sparkled briefly in the dim light, first in the driver's hand, then far into the space between him and the girl. As it flashed inches from her face, Remo saw that it was a steel-tipped mace on a chain. Even lying on the ground wouldn't protect her from a weapon like that.

Remo charged the bike, but it skittered away.

After a few moments, the girl stood up. "He's gone," she said.

"I don't think so." Already he heard the change in the engine that signaled a turn. The bike was coming back for them. "Just get down behind that scrub," Remo said. "Stay as well hidden as you can."

"Okay." She scrambled for the cover of the thin brush growing near the cliff's edge, but her voice became a howl as the earth gave way beneath her and slid like a dead weight with it. She clung to some scrub halfway down the cliff, its nettles digging into her palms. "Remo!" she screamed. "I'm going to fall!"

And now, the motorcycle was nearly on him.

"Hold on," Remo said. "I'm coming after you. Hold on." Inching his way down the sheer cliff, he heard the sound of the engine roaring above him. A cascade of small stones and earth loosened by his hands rolled continuously into Remo's eyes. He could taste the dirt. Just as he reached the girl, he heard the dirt bike's engine click off.

"I'm going to push you up," Remo said. "He's up there, so once you hit ground, just run like hell." He placed one hand around her knee and pushed it upward hard, at an angle so that the girl would land some distance from the boots of the biker immediately above him. There was a thump, and then the frantic running steps of the girl.

The man above Remo did not move.

Suddenly Remo felt foolish hanging stark naked from a cliff with an island version of a Hell's Angel towering above him. "Wanna talk, buddy?" Remo asked.

The biker responded by pulling the steel mace out of his jacket. It whirred to life above his head.

"Well, if that's the way you want it," Remo said. "Don't say I didn't warn you."

A half-smile spread across the biker's face as he lowered the whistling, whirling mace toward Remo. Then, with a motion so swift that the mace seemed to be twirling in · slow motion, Remo caught the weapon as it was coming for him and yanked himself up to ground level. The propulsion of the mace was such that he landed some distance from the biker, who blinked and sputtered, "Hey, mon, I talk. I talk." Remo came up to him slowly. The man backed away. "No. I say I tell—"

"Don't!"

Remo's warning went unheeded and unheard. The biker was already screaming as the loose earth fell below him and cast him bouncing like a rubber ball down the cliff into the whirling waters of the sea.

Fabienne dragged herself to Remo. "You all right?" he asked.

"Yes." She was sobbing. "Remo, was he trying to kill me?"

"Either you or me, sweetheart. We won't know for a while. Anyway, he's gone."

Five

ALBERTO VITTORELLI, the card read in the dim moonlight at the Soubise shipyard. The Dutchman had turned the lights off when he entered the compound. The place was silent except for the ragged grumbling and snoring of the men his mute, Sanchez, had brought for him. He was surprised when a little dark-haired man scrambled from the pile of insensate drunks in the corner and weaved toward him, thrusting his name embossed on white plastic in front of the Dutchman's face.

The card offered by the bruised, groggy man was his official identification for Lordon Lines.

"Do you still work for Lordon?" the Dutchman asked in English. Lordon was an English line whose cruisers regularly docked at Sint Maarten harbor.

The rumpled fellow held his temples with both

hands, as though the Dutchman's voice were deafening. "*Scusi?*" he asked with some difficulty.

The Dutchman changed his language to Italian. "Do you work for the ship?" he asked, pointing to the enormous, light-festooned luxury liner a half-mile out to sea in the harbor.

"*Si, si,*" the Italian said, brightening. In a torrent of emotion, he explained how he had been rolled in an alley by a group of drunken sailors who left him unconscious after stripping his wallet. "I always carry my identification in my vest pocket for just such an emergency, so that I may reboard the ship."

He looked around at the grim, bleak shipyard cluttered with metal truck containers standing in utter darkness. In a far corner of the yard, Vittorelli saw the group of men he had been with when he came to consciousness amid their unwashed bodies and alcoholic fumes. The men were bums, filthy, ragged beggars who moaned softly as they shifted their weight in the corner of the shipyard, oblivious to their unusual surroundings. They were a dramatic contrast from the tall, imperious aristocrat who stood before him, fixing him with cold, light eyes.

"You are from the . . . authorities, *signor?*" Vittorelli asked dubiously.

The Dutchman held down a surge of anger at Sanchez for his blunder. The mute had communicated to him that the night's preparations had been made. He was to have gone to the alleyways and tramp camps of Phillipsburg and Marigot to root out the island's dispossessed for the Dutch-

64

man's use. No one missed these men, who would disappear in the night and never return. When the Dutchman finished with them, their corpses were to be loaded into a forty-foot container and hauled out to deep water, where they would sink, forgotten, into the sea.

Fortunately, the Dutchman did not often require live partners for his practice. The possibility of picking up a victim who *would* be missed and reported was too great. Killing at the yard was rare, but it was still dangerous.

The worst had already happened. An American salvage ship had accidentally found a container loaded with bodies from one of the Dutchman's nights at the yard. He thought, when he had first heard the vessel was in the area, of forcing the ship's crew to abandon their search, but he knew Americans. At the slightest interference, they would search harder, thinking someone wanted to prevent them from locating the remains of the Spanish galleon they were after. So he'd kept to himself and they had found the bodies. Fortunately, he had made sure the box was untraceable to the Soubise Harbor Transportation Corporation by altering some invoices in the office. When the island authorities came to question the executives at the yard, they were shown the inventory records indicating that no containers had been lost or stolen, and they had left satisfied.

But it was not the island authorities who worried the Dutchman. Hours after the container was lifted on board the salvage ship, the Dutchman spotted a fleet of U.S. Army helicopters swarming around the ship. They stayed for some time, then left without questioning anyone on the island. Shortly after the helicopters took off, the salvage ship pulled away from Sint Maarten waters and never returned for the legendary sunken treasure ship. There was no word on the unusual find in any major publication in any language.

Clearly the United States government was somehow involved, but how? America was one of the few countries on earth that had never laid claim to the island. Someone had sent those helicopters in response to the ship's signal. Someone had hushed up the news. And now, someone might be watching to see if it happened again.

"What do you do on the ship?" the Dutchman asked Vittorelli. "Are you important?"

"Important? I?" The Italian spread his hands over his chest. "*Signor,* I assure you that I am of extreme importance. The ship cannot sail without Alberto. Without my services, Lordon's sauce is like river water. Pah!" He spat ceremoniously, if nervously, at a spot as far away from the coldly majestic Dutchman as he could muster.

"Do explain yourself," the Dutchman said. "Briefly."

"Very fast, very fast," Vittorelli whimpered, his hands fluttering like birds' wings at his sides. "*Signor,* I am the *sous-chef* in the ship's kitchen. I make the sauces. If I do not return, nine hundred and twelve passengers will sail tomorrow morning, doomed to eight days of dry salad, naked asparagus, and white spaghetti. I beg you, *signor.* There has been a great mistake."

There was a mistake, all right. A missing *sous-chef* wouldn't force Lordon into a full investigation, but it was still risky. He would have to let the man go.

"My apologies, *signor*," the Dutchman said. "There has been a rash of vandalism at the shipyard recently, which we believe was instigated by some of our own men. We have brought the suspects here for questioning, so as not to involve the police in our internal affairs. You understand."

Vittorelli cast a sidelong glance at the disorderly array of drunks at the far end of the yard. "*Those* are your workers, *signor?*"

The Dutchman's eyes grew even colder. "Perhaps you don't understand," he said softly.

"*Si! Si!* I understand perfectly, *signor*. Perfectly." His beet-red face nodded enthusiastically. "I go now, okay?" With trembling hands he reached for his Lordon identification.

"One more thing, Mr. Vittorelli," the Dutchman said.

"S-s-si?"

"You are not to discuss this episode with anyone. Is that clear?"

"Oh, absolutely."

"Because if you do, you will never set foot on Sint Maarten again."

"You will have no difficulty from me, *signor*. None whatsoever. *Con permiso . . .*"

You groveling little toad, the Dutchman thought.

Vittorelli jumped involuntarily.

"Go," the Dutchman commanded, forcing his eyes away from the Italian and toward the darkness over the Atlantic. The killing picture that began deep in the Dutchman's brain and shot out toward the Italian missed its target. Instead, the spark of loathing exploded harmlessly in the night sky, bursting over the sea like a firecracker. As the burning half-thought dissipated, the Dutchman gave a small sigh of relief. He was beginning, with great effort, to control the destructive force inside him.

Vittorelli shrieked at the sight of the spontaneous display in the sky. He ran at top speed toward the high-voltage fence.

"Stop!" the Dutchman called. "The fence is electrified. I'll let you out."

But the Italian kept running. With a leap, he plastered himself spread-eagled to the wire fence. The charge took him at once, shaking his limbs ferociously. Sparks bristled around his hair, which stood completely on end, and smoke smoldered from his shoes as he gurgled strangled sounds.

The Dutchman kicked him off the fence. Vittorelli's twitching body rolled toward the group of drunks who sat clutching one another in horror as they witnessed his electrocution. The drunks recoiled and scattered, shouting wildly.

It had all gone out of control. The Dutchman would have to stop them all before their noise brought curious onlookers to the yard. But first he would have to get rid of the source of their fright, the gory mass of flesh that still trembled spasmodically nearby. With one hand, he threw Vittorelli's grisly, burned body high over the fence into the ocean beyond, while he trapped a terrified drifter,

68

now stone sober and surprisingly strong, with the other. When Vittorelli hit the water with a resounding splash, the Dutchman turned to the drifter and silenced him with one lethal blow to the windpipe, then dropped him. He was searching for the nearest scream.

It came from an old black man who limped toward the office complex. The Dutchman caught him in the solar plexus with his foot, then split his temple open with two fingers. He killed the others cleanly, seeking them out among the trucks and sandbags where they hid, making sure each kill was unique by striking different blows on each frightened, bewildered victim.

When it was over, he counted the bodies. There were ten, including Vittorelli—the same number Sanchez had brought in earlier. The fragrant tropical air was already beginning to smell of death. The Dutchman opened a refrigerated truck container used for hauling meat and produce, and tossed the bodies inside after removing any personal effects and identification from them. These would be burned in the furnace at the castle.

He closed the door to the container, set its dials, and it whirred into action. The sea slapped at the shore in peaceful rhythm while the motor of the container chilled its terrible cargo. The box would be carried out to sea soon. As soon as the bodies of Remo and Chiun filled it.

Outside the compound, the scrub grass stirred with heavy footsteps. The Dutchman pasted himself to the side of the refrigerated box and watched as the figure drew closer. It walked clumsily, as if the person carried a heavy load. At the gate, the figure held something in its hand that glinted like metal in the moonlight. In a moment, the gate slid open. It was Sanchez.

In his arms was the water-bloated, gray-tinged body of a man in black. Sanchez dropped the body in front of the Dutchman and signaled that he had found him floating between the reefs below the French girl's house.

The Dutchman pulled back his hand and slapped the mute across the face. "For your ineptitude," he spat. The mute stood, expressionless.

"Is the American, Remo, dead?" he asked after a moment.

The mute shook his head.

So. He would have to take them both at once. It would have been better to kill the young one first, but that was a bad gamble at best. No one knew better than the Dutchman how dangerous this American was. Nearly as dangerous as the old man from Sinanju. He had been counting on the thug who now lay dead at his feet to catch Remo off guard, but he should have known that killing either Remo or Chiun was not a job for an ordinary killer. He would have to do it himself.

"So be it," he said quietly.

Sanchez lifted the body into the truck container, already cold with frigid air that frosted the hair and beards of the unlucky drifters inside, and locked the door. At the gate, he slid a metal-striped card into a slot, and the gate opened for them and closed behind them. Two more switches, and the place was once again flooded in bright light. They walked together into the darkness.

"Has any harm come to the girl?" the Dutchman asked.

His head down, the mute signaled "No" with his hands.

After a moment, the Dutchman spoke again. "See that it does."

The mute nodded and was gone.

Six

The porch lights of Remo's villa were on. In the near distance, Remo blinked twice when he saw the opened front door. The doorway seemed to be crammed full of people, as though a busy party were in progress, only there was no sound. No music, no bursts of cocktail laughter, nothing but the drone of the cicadas and the chirping of grasshoppers.

Then he saw one of the figures in the doorway, a black man in a striped shirt, move. It was more a slump than a conscious movement, lodged as the man was between the other people clustered in the frame of the open door. Remo came closer. The man who had moved now slid to the floor, upsetting the balance of the other figures. In one confusing wave, they all tumbled out the door and onto the porch, where they lay inert as broken glass figurines.

"Now what the hell is going on?" Remo said as he stepped over the dead bodies of the toppled partygoers on the porch.

Chiun was inside, frowning, his arms folded across his chest and concealed inside the wide gold brocade sleeves of his robe. "Where have you been?" the old man grumbled, gesturing with a snap of his head at the lifeless forms cluttering the entranceway. "Move this rubble away."

"That's it, huh?" Remo said, kicking a limp arm out of his way in disgust. "Bump off half the men in the village so old Remo, the clean-up man, can come mop up the mess. Well, let me tell you, I've had it up to here with murders today." He mimed a slash across his throat.

"And what of me? The rudeness . . ." Chiun hissed. "Twice in one day have I been coarsely interrupted during the viewing of my beautiful daytime dramas. Emperor Smith, crawling through my window with the agility of a chained bear, is not enough. No. I must also suffer these . . ." His voice rose to a high-pitched shriek as he jounced up and down in a rage. ". . . These murderous hellions, shouting 'Hee Hoo Ha Hee' like hysterical monkeys as they went about their dastardly deed. It is a zoo, this sweltering armpit of an island. Vacation? Hah! Prison would be better. Poverty would be better than this."

"Now, just calm down—"

"Calm?" Chiun's almond eyes were little hazel o's. "You wish me to be calm—I, who have lost the single thread of beauty in life's tormented fabric? I, whose only pleasure in the dimming twilight of my years has now been shattered beyond redemption?"

"Will you get to it? What the hell are you talking about?"

Wordlessly, Chiun glided out of the living room, uttered a small cry of grief, and returned wheeling the television set with its Betamax hookup, which he kept in his bedroom. The blank screen was punctured by a gaping hole, out of which the machine's innards were visible.

"This," the old man said, choking hoarsely. "The lout did not even have the decency to die properly. Kicking, flailing everywhere like a wild chicken." He thrust his hand speculatively into the hole in the glass, then retracted it, wailing high and stridently. "Oh, never again to gaze on Mrs. Wintersheim's troubled countenance. Never to know the dark secret of Skip the podiatrist. And Rad Rex, the kindest of healers, the finest—"

"You've seen those shows a million times," Remo said.

Chiun turned on him, eyes blazing. "And if one sees the Mona Lisa a million times, is it then permissible to destroy her?"

"I'll go into town tomorrow and get you another set," Remo said impatiently.

"Tomorrow?" Chiun bellowed. "Tomorrow? What am I to do tonight?" He glared at the broken television. "This is worthless now, isn't it?"

Remo shrugged. "I guess you could use it for a coffee table if you wanted to. . . ."

"Worthless. Gone forever, the lovely stories that lived within this magic box." He tossed the set

74

into the air like a tennis ball and whacked it across the room, where it embedded itself in the stucco wall.

Remo jumped. "Remember what I said, Chiun. Calm. Let's be . . ."

"I am calm," Chiun hissed as he strode over to the heap of bodies in the doorway and propelled one of the dead men through the picture window with a crash of shattering glass. "Miserable, destructive wretches," he said. He kicked another into the kitchen. The body came to rest at the base of the refrigerator, which crumpled around it. "They have no respect for property," Chiun said, flinging another limp figure upward with a snap of his wrist. The body shot into the ceiling, where it stuck halfway, its corduroy-clad legs hanging limply down like a grotesque chandelier.

"Okay, you've made your point. I'll get rid of the bodies," Remo said, quickly pulling two of the dead men out into the yard. Chiun spun another through the back door, knocking it off its hinges.

"I'm doing it, I'm doing it," Remo shouted from the yard.

"Never will an old man find peace in these violent times," Chiun muttered.

An hour later, Remo had dumped most of the dead into the ocean and returned to the wreckage of the villa.

"Him, too," Chiun said tightly, gesturing with a thumb toward the man in corduroys whose lower half hung suspended from the ceiling.

"Oh. I forgot." Remo tugged gently at the legs, grunting as he tried to pry the body loose. "Hey, what were these guys doing here, anyway? Did you think to ask before you knocked them off?"

Chiun sniffed. "Who knows what lunacy impels men who smash televisions?"

"I mean, were they trying to rob you?"

The old man paused and gave Remo a puzzled look. "Actually, I think they were trying to kill me," he said.

"What for?"

Chiun made a face. "How should I know? The white mind has always been inscrutable. Stupid is always inscrutable."

"These men are all black," Remo said.

"Close enough."

"Well, what'd they do?"

Chiun rolled his eyes in exasperation. "The usual. They came inside, playing with their knives and guns." He swept an open ten-inch switchblade into the bushes with his toe. "They were hooting in that incomprehensible language, and in a moment they had all departed for the Great Void. Except for the one with the dancing feet who smashed my television. By the way, his remains are in the carpet of my bedroom."

"Oh, come on," Remo groaned. He trotted into the room to see. "This is gross," he called over his shoulder as he picked up the rolled-up carpet. "Couldn't you just kill him and leave it at that?"

"*But he broke my television,*" Chiun explained. "Just as Mrs. Wintersheim . . ."

"Yeah, yeah." Too tired to stand on ceremony, Remo hoisted the carpet onto his shoulder and returned to the living room, where he yanked the

76

other body out of the ceiling, with a shower of dust and plaster. The man in the corduroys tumbled to the floor like a sack of cement. "Well, I can't figure it out," Remo said. "Nobody even knows us here, and this makes three times today that someone's tried to ice one of us."

"You, too?" Chiun asked in a tone of voice that immediately struck Remo as too casual.

"Twice," Remo said, eyeing him slowly. "And you know something about it, so speak up. What's going on?"

"I know nothing." Chiun's fingers twitched toward the plaster-covered body. "Take this mad dog away."

Something caught Remo's eye. It was lying on the floor beside the dead man, coated with fallen debris. "This must have fallen out of his pocket," Remo said, picking it up.

It was a plastic card the size of a credit card, only it had no markings on it except for a wide metal band running along its length. "What do you think it is?" Remo asked, turning the card over in his palm.

Chiun snapped it out of his hand irritably. "Clean up this rubbish first," he said. "Later will we solve the riddles of this ill-mannered island." He tossed the card onto an end table while Remo dragged the corpses outside.

There was something strange about this night. Remo felt it as he hauled the dead men toward the cold mist of the ocean. He tossed in the rolled-up carpet.

Well, why shouldn't the night be strange? The

day had been weird enough. Smitty, for one thing, with his transparent talk about taking a vacation on an island near the one that Remo and Chiun were on. Harold W. Smith didn't take vacations, not with his employees, at any rate. Then the murder attempts. Two for Remo and one for Chiun. Something was going on here, and whatever it was, Smith knew about it. Remo was here for a reason, although he couldn't imagine what it was. All he knew was that something lurked on this island paradise, something dark and frightening. Chiun was right. Some vacation.

A rustling sounded in the distance, Remo looked behind his shoulder. Nothing. That was what was strange about this night, he realized as his eyes moved from the night-blackened coastline to the sky. There was no moon. Sometime in the past hour a cloud cover had blotted out the moon and the twinkling stars that were the only light outdoors at night. Without them, the island was as black as the innards of Hell.

The rustling sounded again, closer, with the *pat-pat-pat* of approaching footsteps on the sand. Remo listened. They were coming from the west, the direction he had walked home from. He gathered his thoughts together, trying to remember. West was Fabienne's house and Devil's Mountain and that winding goat-herders' road he had taken with Pierre, and the shipyard with its modern security system. . . .

The shipyard.

Now ·he remembered. When he walked back from Fabienne's, the lights at the shipyard had been off. They had been blazing when he had gone up the winding road with Pierre, but coming back, the place was dark and invisible.

The steps came closer. Whoever was coming was running. As far away as the runner had to be by the sound of his footfalls, Remo could hear out-of-breath panting. He set down the body he was carrying and squatted a hundred feet or so away. Close enough so that he, with the heightened night vision drilled into him over the years, could see the runner before being seen himself.

The running figure came forward at full speed, then fell with a thud over the body of the man in corduroys. The runner got up, explored the body briefly, then let loose with a howling, high-pitched scream. A woman's scream.

Fabienne. Remo ran toward her. She turned tail and dashed madly for the woods, fighting and kicking and squealing like a banshee. She wailed, "No, no!" as Remo finally got her in his grip.

"It's all right. It's me, Remo."

"Remo?" She turned hesitantly. "Oh, Remo." She flooded with tears and held onto him. She was shaking wildly. Her breath came in gulps. "He came for me," she shrieked hysterically, the words tumbling from her between long, hoarse breaths. "In the house . . . after you left. . . . His hands were on my throat . . . going to kill me. . . ."

"Hold on," Remo said. "I'm taking you inside. You can tell me there. You're freezing."

"I had to swim. . . . Sharks . . . afraid of sharks."

"Shhh. You're okay now, little girl." He stroked her wet hair to calm her. When she quieted, he picked her up and carried her into the villa. "You just take it easy till we get you into some dry clothes." He stepped carefully over the pile of rubble in the living room and set her down on a sofa. She was still trembling. Her neck was swollen, and thick bruises circled it like a chain.

Chiun walked in carrying a load of clean towels and a blue silk kimono. "Who is this latest disturbance of the peace?" he asked.

"The woman I went to see tonight. Looks like whoever came after you and me is going for her, too."

After a change of clothing and a stiff shot of Sidonie's rum, Fabienne had stopped shaking and was well enough to talk.

"Thank you," she said, accepting the second glass of island firewater Remo offered her. Her eyes widened as she took in the decimated room. "He's been here, too," she said. She lowered her head in despair.

"Some were, but they weren't a lot of trouble," Remo said soothingly. He saw her focus on the television planted in the wall and added quickly, "They didn't do that. That's just Chiun's idea of interior decorating."

"Tell us what happened," Chiun said. Again, his interest triggered Remo's suspicions.

Fabienne downed the rest of her drink. A lone tear trickled down her cheek. "Oh, I'm so sorry you had to be involved. Both of you."

"Perhaps we are involved more than you think,"

Chiun said. "Tell us what you can. Without tears, please."

"He came for me after Remo left," she said. "I was asleep. He got on top of me and tried to strangle me." She touched the bruises on her neck with a wince of pain. "There was nothing near my bed except for a candle, but it was all I had. I got hold of it somehow and poked him in the eye, I think. He jumped, and I managed to squirm away. It was horrible." She slapped both hands over her eyes, as though trying to erase the memory.

"Go on," Remo said gently.

"I got out of the house and ran down the back roads to the shore. He followed me. He was very close. He would have got me for certain if the clouds hadn't come in so quickly. When the moon disappeared, it became dark very suddenly. I backtracked toward the woods, and I heard him stop behind me. I think he became confused when he couldn't see me. So I crouched down behind a rock and listened. He was moving slowly, listening for me, too. Then I saw some stones nearby. I picked up a few of them and threw them into the woods. He followed them, *merci à Dieu.*"

"And you came here."

"Not directly. He would have heard me. Instead, I crawled as quietly as I could back to the beach and got in the water. It was totally dark by then. I don't think he saw me, but I went out as far as I dared, just to be sure. Sharks come to these waters at night. I was frightened that one would come after me, but I couldn't risk getting back onto land. I knew he would be looking for me there, waiting. I swam to about a kilometer from here, and ran the rest of the way."

Remo made a face. "What I can't figure out is, why would this person—whoever he is—want to kill you?"

She looked at him, her mouth turned downward in bitter irony. "Oh, didn't I tell you? I know who he is. The mute. The Dutchman's servant."

Remo and Chiun exchanged a glance. "Perhaps you would like to rest," Chiun said. "We have time for these matters tomorrow."

She nodded. "I suppose you're right. Thank you."

Remo led her to his bedroom. He came back in a few minutes to find Chiun lost in thought in front of the broken window.

"I'll be right back," Remo said. "I still have to get rid of one of the guys you sent to Happy Land."

"Take me to the body," Chiun said.

Near the shore, Remo picked up the man in corduroys by the armpits. "I've been taking them over to that cliff and tossing them in," he said, nodding toward the darkness. "The water's pretty deep there—"

"Break his arm," Chiun said.

"What?"

"Break his arm. The forearm."

Remo dropped the body with a sigh. "Now, isn't this going a little far? I mean, maybe they did break your T.V., but the poor sucker's already dead. . . ."

"Arguments, always arguments," Chiun snapped.

"Is it always so difficult for you to fulfill the simplest request? Do you find it so impossible . . ."

The arm broke with a snap.

"Ah," Chiun said. "A little respect, at last." He picked up the dead man's arm and examined the break with his fingers. "Is this your best attack?" he asked crisply.

Remo rolled his eyes. "Want me to go down to the morgue and practice?"

"Break the other arm."

"Aw, come *on*."

"Do as I say."

Remo picked up the other arm reluctantly. "I feel like a ghoul."

Chiun glared at him, the hazel eyes glinting threateningly in the darkness.

He broke the second arm with a quick chop. Chiun fluttered over to feel the break. Amid a series of muttered "hmmms" and "ahs," he bounced from one side of the body to the other, scrutinizing the new breaks. "Just as I thought," he declared finally. He dismissed Remo with a wave of his hand. "You may dispose of this carrion now."

"Wait just a freaking minute. Now that I've broken both arms of a corpse, would you mind telling me what is just as you thought?"

Chiun sputtered. "I'm sorry, Remo. I try but you just have no brains. Any idiot could see why I asked you to break his arms."

"Not any idiot," Remo said hotly.

"To see if your elbow was bent," Chiun shrieked.

Remo stepped back, dumbstruck. Chiun turned gracefully back toward the villa.

"Was it?" Remo asked so softly, he could barely hear it himself.

Chiun cackled from afar. "Yes, of course. Your elbow is always bent." He hooted with delight. He was going to sleep well tonight, very well indeed. He had the proof he needed now. Emperor Smith was a white fool to think that Remo could have killed the men in the photographs he carried. Now Chiun could confirm Remo's innocence. Smith could compare the results of Remo's attack and see that they were different from those in the picture. The man who slew those unfortunates in the sunken truck did not bend his elbow when he worked. He did not make small mistakes. Only big ones.

His biggest was to forward a letter that should have remained locked in the tomb of the past.

In his room, Chiun rolled out his tatami sleeping mat and prepared for deep rest. He would need it, for tomorrow he would do battle with a ghost.

A ghost more deadly and evil than any man.

Seven

Mrs. Hank Cobb gave her husband's arm a squeeze as they strolled in the brisk morning air on the second-class deck of the *Coppelia*. On the island a half-mile away, graceful palms waved good-bye while the ship's mighty foghorn sounded. As usual when leaving port, Mrs. Cobb cried.

"There, there," her husband said, patting her hand paternally, even though his lips betrayed a smile of pleasure and pride. "Not a bad second honeymoon, wouldn't you say, Emily?"

Emily Cobb gently kissed the white-haired, stoop-shouldered man at her side. "Second? I didn't know the first one was over," she said, causing the man she had lived with for twenty-five years to blush like a schoolboy. Together they stood on deck, waving back to the silent palms, their new Sony Trinitron and Swedish Valpox stereo safely crated below.

Near the ship, something bobbed momentarily to the surface before being engulfed again by the waves. "What's that?" Mrs. Cobb asked, pointing to the object.

"A log, I think, or a broken telephone pole," Mr. Cobb answered thoughtfully. "Then again, it couldn't be a telephone pole. I haven't seen any of those here. Come to think of it, I haven't seen any trees that big around in the whole darned Caribbean, have you?"

Mrs. Cobb felt an uneasy wobbling in her stomach. "It . . . it doesn't really look like a tree," she said hesitantly.

"Well, then maybe it's something off the ship."

The object came to the surface again, dark and shining in the bright reflection of the sun on the ocean.

"Hank . . . Hank," she cried low, her fingers clutching her husband's coat in a terrified grip. Mr. Cobb struggled with her while he peered over his glasses at the thing floating on the surface of the water, the dun-colored item where his wife's attention was so desperately riveted.

"Damn bifocals," he muttered. "Emily, for God's sake, what's the matter?" He turned to her quickly. "You feel all right, don't you, dear?"

And Mrs. Cobb opened her mouth automatically to assure Mr. Cobb that she was feeling just fine, but at that moment the thing drifted alongside the ship and opened its eyes in its charred skull. Its teeth flashed white, as though belonging to a corpse that had risen from some dank and ancient grave, and its blood trailed behind it in a ribbon. And Emily Cobb shattered the silence on deck with the most horrifying sound she had ever uttered.

She screamed, rooted to the spot where she stood, as the cruise director turned smiling toward her. She screamed as his smile disintegrated into a hideous grimace and he called for help on his walkie-talkie. She screamed as a tangle of crewmen flooded around her with ropes and a lifeboat and went scurrying down the ladder to sea level. And she screamed when the ship's surgeon appeared, bleary and frantic, to check her pulse and command her husband in boozy tones to take her to their cabin as the crewmen shouted and heaved their blackened cargo into the lifeboat below.

In her cabin, Mrs. Cobb lay on her small bunk, trying to remember. Her husband's soothing, frightened words washed over her like surf. That terrible burned body, those eyes that opened suddenly like a porcelain doll's . . .

On deck, Dr. Matthew Caswell held back a wave of revulsion as the sailors dumped the blackened thing that had once been a man onto a stretcher and followed the doctor into the infirmary. Heat attacks were not uncommon on board cruisers the size of the *Coppelia*. Strokes, food poisoning, broken arms and legs, even a couple of premature births. But nothing like this. He hoped the captain had already radioed the island police for a boat to take the vile-smelling cadaver in front of him to the morgue before he upchucked his breakfast of two bloody Marys and a beer chaser.

He set his nurse, retching, to cutting the body's clothes off as he attended to the formalities of confirming death. The first of the formalities was to down half the hip flask he carried. All else were technicalities.

Even through his whiskey haze, Caswell saw that an autopsy was in order back on the island. Third-degree burns throughout, severe loss of blood, and an amputated leg on top of it all. Newly amputated, too, by the looks of it: Undoubtedly a shark. Long tendrils of flesh hung from the top of the leg near the hip, and the bone had been snapped. The poor fellow had taken a long time to die.

Holding his breath, Caswell placed his stethoscope against the man's chest, making a mental note to replace the instrument at the next port, along with the hip flask, which was far too small.

"Wait a minute," he said half to himself.

"I've found some identification, Doctor."

"Quiet."

Oh, no. It couldn't be. It was next to impossible.

"Call the captain," he ordered. "Tell him to come here."

But it was true. The doctor rushed frantically to get a proper tourniquet on the leg, then wheeled out an I.V. with a pint of plasma.

Why me, he moaned inwardly, his hands trembling. Matthew Caswell hadn't operated in years. Of all the places on earth for a dead-serious medical emergency to turn up, why did it have to be here? With him? "I'm sorry," Caswell whispered to the barely breathing remains of the stranger who was fated to die under Dr. Matthew Caswell's unsteady knife. "I'm so terribly sorry, mister. You've been through so much. You deserve better."

Then a strange thing happened. The burned man on the table opened one blackened eyelid. He held his gaze on the doctor for a long moment before lapsing back into unconsciousness.

He saw me, the doctor thought. He saw, and he knows what I am. "I was a good surgeon once," Caswell said aloud. Then he ran to the toilet and vomited the entire morning's intake of vodka and beer and rye into the ship's tank.

The captain entered without knocking, a handsome, efficient-looking man in his forties who was clearly impatient to get rid of the body and continue the cruise. "What is it?" he snapped.

"This man's alive," Caswell said, spitting into the sink.

"Oh, Jesus Christ."

"He can't be moved. He'll have to stay here until I can . . ." The doctor shivered involuntarily. ". . . Can operate on his leg. Shark damage, and he's got extensive electrical burns. You can see the diamond-shaped pattern on his palms and thigh. It was probably a fence. Also, he's in shock. He'll need skin grafts and a lot of blood. . . ."

"*You're* going to operate?" the captain sneered. "Well, that shouldn't take long."

The doctor ignored him. "I can perform the operation in a few hours, but I'll need a small team from the island, a couple of surgeons and—"

"Don't make me laugh, Caswell."

". . . And three or four good nurses. And some plasma, at least six pints. They can take him back to the hospital when I'm through."

The captain smiled indulgently, a cruel smile reserved for rummies and other washouts who tried to sound like they knew what they were doing.

Well, Caswell thought, I can't say I didn't earn the man's disrespect.

"How many hours are we talking about?"

The doctor wiped his forehead with the back of his hand as he helped the nurse assemble his instruments. "I don't know. Three or four, unless he dies. Look, I've got to hurry. Please try to get me some help, Captain."

"Three or four hours," the captain muttered. "The passengers'll miss half a day in Jamaica."

"Captain, please. Do as you like, but you must leave now. I've got to scrub."

The captain turned with a disgusted sigh.

"I need that team, sir."

At that moment, Mrs. Hank Cobb sat bolt upright in her bunk, her eyes wide and staring.

"Lie down, Emily. I told the doctor—"

"We *know* that man, Hank," she shrilled.

"What man? Oh, Emily, not that—that thing down there."

"Those eyes," she screamed. "Those teeth!"

"Please, dear—"

90

"He's the *cook*! The ship's cook. He gave me the recipe for that celery seed dressing, don't you remember?"

Hank Cobb searched his memory. "The cook . . ."

Half a city block away, in the ship's infirmary, Alberto Vittorelli was fading back out of his brief episode of consciousness. The black wall of the ship—how did the *ship* appear? The woman screaming, the bobbing faces all around him, their wet hair plastered to their heads, the gentleman in the white suit moving hurriedly above him now, his expression of worry so deeply graven on his face that it seemed almost comical.

The antiseptic-smelling white room began to swirl around him. Of course they had come to rescue him. Without Vittorelli, the ship would sail with no sauces. He closed his eyes to the whirling, darkening place, its lone occupant the worried gentleman in white. But the spinning continued inside Vittorelli like a tight, diminishing merry-go-round. The riders on the merry-go-round (Faster! round and round it went, faster and faster!) were the men in the sea with him, their sailor uniforms bright in the dark water, the sailors and the screaming woman and the worried gentleman in white. And at the center of it all, so small now, small and disappearing, was another face, cold and commanding, swept by yellow hair, lit by the palest ice-blue eyes, a face he would never forget. . . .

Eight

The next morning was Sunday. Remo sprang awake to a deafening howl, the thunder of heavy, bewildered footsteps, and the clanking of glasses and ice cubes. He wrapped a towel around himself and headed for the kitchen, but Sidonie intercepted him just outside the bedroom.

"What you do out there?" the housekeeper accused, her eyes pinched into little black marbles. "This place a mess."

"We had visitors last night," Remo said lamely.

Sidonie craned her neck past him into the bedroom, where Fabienne was groaning awake, her hand held to her throbbing forehead. "Land sake, boy," Sidonie gasped, stepping backward in indignation. "What for you got her in your bed?"

Remo passed up the obvious explanation in view of the fact that Sidonie was a friend of the girl's, and also because she had to weigh in at over 225 and already had a couple of belts of rum in her. "She's been hurt," he said.

Sidonie waddled tentatively into the room, her ice cubes tinkling in her glass as she swayed her heavy bulk toward the girl in the bed. When she saw the chain of bruises around Fabienne's throat, she placed her hand over her heart, tossed down the full glass of rum, and waddled menacingly back toward Remo. "You do that, white boy?" she growled.

"Come on, Sidonie. Why would I do that?"

She pressed her face close to his, rum fumes invading his nostrils like bayonets. "Maybe underneath that soft white skin, you a mad dog." She lifted an eyebrow.

"Why don't you ask her?"

"Maybe she lie?"

"Oh, good grief," Remo said.

"Maybe she like it." She smiled wickedly.

"Sidonie." Fabienne's voice brought the huge woman running. Remo exhaled gratefully.

"Who do this to you, girl?" she asked, pressing the girl's face into her mammoth bosom. "You tell Sidonie, she going fix his butt good."

Fabienne coughed to bring her voice above a whisper. "It was the mute, Sidonie. The Dutchman's mute."

The black woman's eyes closed as she sucked in air noisily. With two fingers she gave the sign of the Evil Eye to ward off demons.

"You know I'm getting tired of all this crap," Remo said. "Any mention of this Dutchman character around here, and everyone gets scared out of their bloomers. It is to puke."

"Do not mock him," Sidonie warned. "He hear you. He is the Evil One. He knows."

"Oh, bull fat," Remo said. "I'm going up to that castle on the mountain today and haul that mute, or whatever he is, down to the police station. And if the Dutchman doesn't like it, I'm going to pop his cork."

"Do not speak so quickly, Remo." Chiun stood behind him, glittering in a ceremonial robe of teal-blue brocade.

"See, he know," Sidonie said, gravitating toward Chiun, whom she showered with affectionate pats and clucks. "You look real fine today, Mr. Chiun," she said sweetly. She turned back to Remo, scowling. "This white boy, he come out wearing a towel around them skinny legs, him with a girl in his bed."

"I wish I could have been spared the sight," Chiun said. "And I'm sorry for the mess Remo made here last night. We were attacked by hoodlums last night. They broke my television."

"That's a shame, Mr. Chiun. I'll have the place fixed up in no time."

"Can you replace my television?" he asked hopefully.

"You just leave it to me. You going to teach that trash what beat up Fabienne a lesson?"

"Yes. His last lesson," Chiun said coldly.

There was a loud knocking at the door. "What fool come visiting this time of day?" Sidonie mumbled as she lumbered toward the front entrance.

94

"Something special going on today?" Remo asked Chiun, who was arranging the elaborate folds of his ceremonial robe. Chiun shrugged. "You're not going to tell me, are you?" Remo said, fingering the cloth of the kimono.

"There is no need for you to know."

Sidonie's loud whisper wafted toward them. "No," she hissed, stomping. "I ain't giving you no hundred dollah. You never give back the last fifty you borrowed."

"Sidonie, baby," Pierre's smooth voice cooed. "It the truck. She broke. I got to have the money, or I go out of business."

"Too bad for you, then. You got to go to work now like an honest man."

"Who goes?" Chiun called.

"It only Pierre," Sidonie said. "I telling him to leave now. You hear that, boy?"

Remo and Chiun walked into the living room.

"Mister Remo." Pierre nodded. "I come to talk to Fabienne, if she here."

"Hah!" Sidonie grunted. "You come to rob me again."

Pierre ignored her. "I been most everywhere on the island," he said, "looking for her. I got to give her some bad news."

"She's here, but she's not feeling well," Remo said. "Maybe you can tell me."

"Well . . ." He shuffled his feet. "It not good. I seen her house today. It wrecked. Windows smashed, mud all over the door, everything. Look like somebody get real mad, tear the place up."

"It must have been the mute," Remo mused.

95

Pierre's eyes bulged. "The Dutchman's mute?" he said in a strangled squeak.

"Shut up, you nosy no-account . . ."

Pierre gasped. Something was lying on the end table near the sofa. He took a few hesitant steps and picked up the white plastic card that had fallen from the shirt of the dead man when Remo yanked him from the ceiling. "Dis yours?" he asked tentatively.

"Ain't none of your business," Sidonie snapped.

"It is nothing," Chiun said.

"How do you know?" Remo asked, irritated. "We don't even know what it is."

"It the gate-opener," Pierre said softly.

"The gate-opener?"

"It is inconsequential," Chiun said. He pointed Pierre toward the door. "Come again another time. Call first."

"Like maybe next year," Sidonie growled.

"What gate does it open?" Remo asked.

Pierre looked from Remo's face to Chiun's. The old man was tense and angry. "Uh . . . it not important. Like the man say."

"What gate, Pierre?" Remo glided in front of him, locking into the black man's eyes.

"The gate to the shipyard," Pierre admitted, looking at his shoes. "My cousin had one when he work for the Dutchman a while back. He stick it in the gate, and the fence lose electricity. Dat how you get in the shipyard."

"Does your cousin still work there?" Remo asked.

"Naw. Nobody work there long. The Dutchman

don't keep nobody long enough to know nothing. My cousin never even seen the Dutchman. Me neither."

Remo took the card and turned it over in his palm. The shipyard. Everything pointed to the shipyard. And the Dutchman.

"You'd better leave now," Chiun told Pierre. His jaw was clenching.

"Sure thing," Pierre answered with a two-finger salute. "Oh, one more thing, Mr. Remo. My truck. She broke, and—"

"Git!" Sidonie roared. She grabbed him by the shoulder and shook him until his head rolled. "Don't you be bothering the tourists with your cheatin' and lyin'. Git now and don't come back!" She tossed him out the door. He staggered a few feet, regained his balance with a grunt and a hateful backward glance, and headed off.

"What was that about?" Remo asked as he put the card back on the end table.

Sidonie chuckled. "He be bothering everyone on the island to lend him money, but nobody trust Pierre. He never give it back. I throw him out before he try you."

"Oh." It always surprised Remo that money was considered so valuable to most people. He himself had all the money he ever needed, thanks to the good graces of Harold W. Smith, who kept him supplied with cash. Not that he needed much. A man who was officially dead and worked as a government assassin didn't have much use for shiny cars or big homes or a fancy wardrobe. He didn't eat in restaurants, didn't have hobbies, had no family to support. Except for the fact that his physical organism was one of the two best in the world, he was, in worldly matters at least, dead. He had no more use for the money he carried than a corpse in a grave had for credit cards.

He pulled a roll of bills from his pocket and peeled off two fifties. "Give this to Pierre the next time you see him," he said tonelessly. "I guess he can use it. Here, take a hundred for yourself, too."

"Mr. Remo—"

"Where's Chiun?" The old man had vanished. Remo took a quick look around the house, although he knew Chiun wouldn't be there. He had known about the card, and for some reason he had kept it from Remo. The end table where he had placed the card was empty. Right now the old Oriental would be making his way, swiftly and silently, toward a place where Remo was not invited.

"Take care of the girl," Remo said on his way out the door.

He reached the shipyard in a few minutes at a dead run, passing near a tangled swamp where bamboo grew in tall shoots. The fence surrounding the yard hummed with its charge of deadly high voltage. Chiun was nowhere in sight. Remo doubled back to the swamp, hacked off a long bamboo pole, then carried it back to the fence and vaulted over.

"Chiun," he called.

"I am here," a voice came from the interior of the shipyard. Chiun was standing near some battered truck bodies, his hands tucked into the sleeves of his robe. He said, "Go home, Remo. This is not your affair."

"I just want to know what the hell's going on here. Since we started this so-called vacation, I've been shot at, hung off a cliff, maced, and told to break the arms of a dead man. Now Fabienne's been half strangled, our house is a disaster, and here you are in the middle of a shipyard in a god-damn ceremonial robe. You can't expect me to just turn around now and go home."

Chiun shrugged. "Then stay. But remember. When the time comes, what we will encounter is my business, not yours."

"Maybe," Remo said.

Chiun withdrew one slender hand from his sleeve and swung over the blood-stained door to the refrigerated truck container beside him. He was silent as Remo peered in.

Inside, nine bodies lay sprawled in grotesque positions. Icicles hung from their mouths and eyes, where their last dribblings had frozen, and their shabby clothes lay in stiff folds around them, stuck to the metal walls and floor. The frigid air inside the container smelled like a meat freezer, the stale odors of flesh and steel mixing together as the container's motor whirred unceasingly.

"Did they freeze to death?" Remo asked.

"Look closer. Look at their wounds."

Remo stepped up into the truck and examined the stiff bodies. "This isn't real," he said, his breath turning the ends of his hair white with new frost. "They were all killed in hand-to-hand combat."

"Karate does not kill this way," Chiun said, stepping into the truck. "That is hand-to-hand. So is atemi-waza, aikido, bando and t'ai chi chuan, but those methods were not used on these men."

Remo shook his head. "It's weird. It looks like one of us killed them."

Chiun sniffed. "It could hardly have been I," he said. "Does this look like perfect technique? But the work is of Sinanju."

Remo stared at him for a long moment, incredulous. "You don't think I did it, do you?" he asked finally.

"Emperor Smith thinks you did. Another truck filled with bodies slain in this manner was found in the ocean. He ordered me to kill you. Naturally, I was interested to see more of this work. The style is quite masterful."

"He ordered *what*?"

"He ordered me to kill you. That is part of my agreement, you know. A contract is a contract."

"But . . . but I didn't do it," Remo stammered. "I've never even been here before. . . ."

"Stop babbling," Chiun snapped. He jumped off the end of the truck to the ground, his robe billowing. "Of course you didn't do it. This is not the work of a bent elbow. Only one highly skilled in the art of Sinanju could kill this way. A clod could never achieve such skill." He waved Remo out and shut the door.

"Wait till I get my hands on Smith. That C.I.A. looney."

"There is no need for spitefulness," Chiun said calmly. "In this truck is more than enough evidence to vindicate you in Emperor Smith's eyes. That was why I had to come here first."

"First? Before what?"

"Before confronting the killer of those men in the truck."

"But I thought we were the only two people alive who still practiced Sinanju," Remo said.

"Alive, yes." Chiun reached into the folds of his robe and pulled out the yellowed scrap of paper bearing three Korean characters. "I knew you were not the killer when I received this."

" 'I live again,' " Remo whispered.

"One who is dead has passed the knowledge of Sinanju on to another." Chiun folded the paper and replaced it in his robe.

"Nuihc?" Remo whispered. "But he's dead. I saw him die."

"He has left an heir. Through him, as his message says, Nuihc and his infamy live again." Chiun looked up toward the castle.

High above the desolate shipyard, its white turrets shone in the morning light. And within its stone walls, a legacy of destruction and evil waited for its moment of triumph.

Nine

Below the Dutchman's castle, perched on a rocky outcropping, Pierre lowered his binoculars after the young American and the old Oriental stepped out of the truck body in the shipyard. Ordinary tourists to Sint Maarten didn't go around stealing magnetic cards and snooping in the shipyard compound on Sunday. The American, Remo, had put on a show of ignorance about the card, but the old man knew.

Something was going on, all right. Fabienne "wasn't feeling well" all of a sudden after meeting Remo, and the Dutchman's mute had gone through her house like a hurricane. Not to mention the shots fired at his own truck yesterday. Whoever the Dutchman was, he had something to do with the two figures in the shipyard below.

And those two men were up to something very fishy.

He toyed with the binoculars hanging around his neck. This information would be worth something to the Dutchman, maybe enough to fix the truck. Still, it meant climbing Devil's Mountain and facing the Dutchman himself. . . .

Pierre scrambled down the crumbling path that led back to the village of Marigot. No, nothing was worth the terrors of Devil's Mountain. White folks' business was their own. He would go into town, borrow the price of a Red Stripe beer, and forget all about it.

Still, the possibility of making a quick hundred nagged at him as he walked, ever more slowly, down the hill. Five minutes inside the Dutchman's castle. That was all it would take, and Pierre would have a crisp new C-note in his pocket for his truck. Maybe the Dutchman would give him more than a hundred in gratitude for learning about the two men in his shipyard. Man, they'd change their tune down in Gus's Grotto when Pierre LeFevre walked in and ordered drinks for the house. Those boys would think twice about refusing him the next time he was hurting for change.

The legend was that the Dutchman brought down madness upon whoever looked on him.

A cache of small stones beneath Pierre's left foot gave way. Dancing and windmilling his arms, he managed to stay upright. Breathing hard, Pierre spit twice on the ground and formed the symbol of the Evil Eye with his fingers. *Okay, okay. I ain't going nowhere but Marigot, boss.*

It was going to be a scorcher today. Already the air hung in a damp curtain of mist that would melt and sizzle the island like pork rind by noon. Houses began to appear here and there along the dirt path that had widened into a passable road leading straight to Marigot. *Red Stripe'll sure taste fine, money or no money, even though it's a stupid legend made up by ignorant islanders who believe any damn foolish thing they hear. . . .*

Cool it, Pierre, a voice inside him said. You don't need no hundred dollars that bad.

Oh, yes I do. And the Dutchman's what can give it to me, if only I wasn't such a chickenshit. And lookee here, a Willys Jeep right here on the road with the keys in the ignition and a ten-gallon can of gas in the back.

He walked around the Jeep checking for flats. Nope, all good tires, and even a crowbar on the back seat. *That Dutchman try to mess with Pierre, I gonna give it to him straight between the eyes. . . .*

Somebody owns this car, the faint inner voice said.

So? I give it back. Just don't want to go up Devil's Mountain on foot.

You can't drive away from the devil, the voice said. It was barely audible.

"You watch me," Pierre said out loud as he climbed in the Jeep and gunned the engine to life. He sang. "Hey pretty baby, can you come out tonight, come out tonight, come out tonight?"

The Jeep skidded fitfully up the winding road and onto another, smoother path lined with tall shade trees. *Easy riding, this road,* Pierre thought as he maneuvered the machine up the dark stillness of Devil's Mountain.

Ten

"So the Dutchman's hooked up with dear, departed Nuihc. The only thing I don't understand is, why did he wait so long to contact us?"

Chiun flashed him an irritated glance. "That is hardly the only thing you don't understand, brainless one." He held up a long index finger. "Point one. This Dutchman person has not contacted *us*. Through Nuihc's letter, he has contacted *me*, and me alone."

"I suppose trying to bump me off twice doesn't count as contact," Remo said sarcastically. Chiun ignored him.

"Point two. The killings in the truck are the work of a young man. Strength and skill without complete control. I have undoubtedly surprised the Dutchman by coming upon his island. He is not yet prepared to face me."

"I didn't think he'd be much of a threat—"

"Point three. This is an assassin of remarkable talent. Remember, our last confrontation with Nuihc was years ago. This boy has trained himself in the finer points of Sinanju. Marvelous." He shook his head in admiration.

Remo reddened. "You sound like you'd rather adopt him than kill him."

"It is always terrible to destroy something of worth," Chiun said. "A fine assassin. From good stock, probably, not some rubbish of the streets."

They neared the entrance to the compound's electric fence. Chiun handed Remo the metal-banded card. "Oh, to train a talent such as his. To nurture such enormous ability in one so young." Chiun's eyes took on a faraway look.

"I don't think he's so hot," Remo said.

"He has tremendous self-discipline."

"His mother wears combat boots." Remo jabbed the card into the slot and kicked at the gate.

The shock shot him twenty feet backward. Remo sat up on the ground with his scalp tingling and his ears ringing. He approached the fence again, holding his hands a fraction of an inch away from the wire mesh. The hairs on his arms stood on end, and the fence emitted a low, continuous hum.

"The power's still on," Remo said. He slid the card in and out of the slot. "Something's gone wrong."

There was another sound, a soft, zipping electronic noise. Remo and Chiun both turned in time to see a metal panel slide open in the corner of the fence. Behind the panel protruded a black six-foot cube with a refrigeration motor attached. Out of the box slithered a nine-foot python.

"Your Dutchman's a real prince, all right," Remo said.

Four more snakes, sickly-white cobras, sped out of the box. They raced unerringly toward the two men.

"Give me the white card," Chiun said softly. He took it between two fingers and snapped it toward the cobras. One of the white snakes split in half, its tail dancing on the ground. The other cobras lunged at its head, their fangs, exposed and dripping. "Now get us out of here," Chiun whispered.

"Why do I always get the hard part?" Remo muttered. He looked around. The bamboo pole he had used to vault over the fence was on the other side. There was nothing movable in the trucking area except trucks.

A truck. It was bulky, but it would have to do. Remo ran in a quick zigzag pattern to one of the inert truck bodies. The giant python noticed the movement and followed the same meandering route. Remo knew he had to work fast. With the snake close behind, he wouldn't have time to drag the unwheeled truck over to the fence. He would have to transport it in an instant, before the python had time to get a grip on his limbs and crush them like cobwebs.

At the far end of the fence, Chiun raced back and forth at dizzying speed. The three remaining cobras followed him with their dolls' eyes, hypnotized, their necks distended with venom.

There was no way to move the truck body. Remo's mind raced. What happened normally when they had to be moved? Well, first they had to be . . . He slapped his forehead. Of course! How could he be so stupid? They had to be *lifted*. He ran toward the compound's one building. On the far side he found what he was looking for. A crane.

He eased in the throttle, and the great machine began to inch forward. Ahead, he could see Chiun still surrounded by cobras, his back to the fence. The levers to Remo's right controlled the movements of the crane. It dipped and rose and swung experimentally as he tried them all out, heading faster now toward the high-voltage wire.

Then his vision was all but obliterated by the shiny, sleek body of the python as it draped itself over the windscreen, its reptilian head searching for him.

Remo fought back the impulse to remove the snake then and there. The crane had to get close enough to Chiun to lift him out of danger, and Chiun's luck with the dazed cobras would last only as long as he kept up his exhausting speed. But with the python covering Remo's line of sight in the cab, the crane could scrape the fence and force an electric charge big enough to explode both the crane and its driver.

He pressed forward. "Tell me when to stop," he yelled. He maneuvered the crane upward. Its chain swung wildly. Although he couldn't see it, Remo knew that the hook at the end of the chain was suspended somewhere near Chiun's head. If he came too close, Chiun would be impaled at about the same time Remo began to fry.

"Closer?" Remo shouted.

There was no answer. The machine moved forward. The snake on the crane's windshield slithered into the cab and wrapped itself around Remo's leg.

"Halt!" Chiun yelled.

With all the discipline he could muster, Remo shut down the throttle as the python hissed itself into a huge coil from his ankle to his thigh.

Chiun leaped high into the air, lighting on the hook of the crane's chain. At the instant he moved, the hypnotized cobras lunged at the spot where Chiun had been. Their fangs grasped the metal fence in a grip of death as their bodies jiggled and waved like ribbons in the breeze. The doll eyes turned milky white, their bodies charred and blackened in seconds. Still they hung onto the deadly steel wire, their jaws lodged in the mesh.

"Move this over the fence," Chiun demanded. "Climb up here."

Sweat poured from Remo's brow. He slammed his fists into the python's rubbery body. With each blow, the snake coiled more tightly. His foot was already throbbing and numb. If he could only get to its head. . . . But the snake's head was tucked securely beneath Remo's thigh, inching toward his groin.

"Remo!"

Get . . . Chiun . . . out, Remo told himself. He would deal with the snake when he could. He raised the crane and swung it over the fence. Chiun rode the hook to the far side of the compound, then jumped off, his robes billowing gaily. He was safe.

Remo rolled out of the cab onto the ground, the python around his leg shifting at lightning speed to envelope his entire body. Now, Remo said to himself as the snake's head darted in front of him. Now. He grabbed the knob with both hands and twisted violently to smash it on the ground. The coils loosened suddenly. Remo pulled himself free, his leg still pounding, and limped to the base of the crane.

The snake periscoped its head unevenly. A shudder ran through its tunnel body. It convulsed once, then lay still.

At the top of the crane, Remo pulled his hurt leg up close to his torso and vaulted in a triple somersault to the sandy earth below. Lying quietly where he landed, he smelled something ripe and burning. He turned toward the fence. The three sizzling cobras were turning into smoking skeletons, their flesh burned to ashes.

"Very slow," Chiun clucked above him. "I do not understand. I am the one surrounded by snakes. I am the one in mortal danger. You had only to operate that ridiculous prehistoric machine. And yet you dawdle coming over the fence. You lie here, feigning exhaustion. One would think *you* had been the one to confront death." His jaw snapped angrily.

111

"I've got to rest a minute," Remo said, wincing. The feeling was coming back into his damaged leg. He tried to squeeze his toes together. His muscles cramped spasmodically.

"I shudder to think what would have happened if a snake had come after *you*." Chiun snorted triumphantly. "You are growing soft, Remo. But perhaps it is not your fault. Perhaps your training began too late. Perhaps your natural ability is limited."

"Perhaps you piss me off, Little Father," Remo said.

"Now, with the Dutchman. Ah, there is a pupil. Young, powerful, intelligent—"

"He just tried to murder you."

"And would have succeeded, were it not for my uncanny timing and quick reflexes."

"Thanks. Glad to know I could be of help."

"Do you think that if the Dutchman were in your place now he would be resting slothfully on the grass? Never. He would be inquiring as to my well-being. He would be concerned over any possible injury to my person. He would . . ."

"He would try to kill you again," Remo said disgustedly. "Can it, Chiun. Let's go." He pulled himself shakily to his feet and limped alongside Chiun.

"He would not be ungrateful and inconsiderate, like some pupils of low talent."

Remo clenched his teeth together. "Look, if you think I'm so inferior to that murdering maniac, why don't you just team up with him and leave me alone?"

Chiun's eyes glistened. "Really? Do you mean that, Remo?" he asked hopefully.

Remo stopped walking. "Sure, if that's what you want. Nobody said you were stuck with me for life." He spoke quietly. Any louder and he might not have been able to control the wobble in his voice.

Hesitantly Chiun smiled, then nodded. "Perhaps I shall speak with him," he said. "I hope you are not offended."

Remo waved him away.

"Very well," Chiun said, obviously pleased. He took a couple of steps backward, away from Remo.

"Chiun?"

"Yes?"

"I did fight with a snake back there. The python."

Chiun smiled. "Of course," he said. "But you are a Master of Sinanju. A snake is but a snake." Chiun turned and walked away toward the castle on Devil's Mountain. He bounced merrily as he walked, his blue ceremonial robe fluttering gaily in the breeze. "Still. Think of it. The Dutchman. Someone trainable, at last. I will remember you fondly, Remo."

"Blow it out your ears, Little Father," Remo said as Chiun walked out of his life.

Remo sat on the ground.

"Trainable," he muttered. Chiun was climbing Devil's Mountain, growing small in the distance. The ingrate. Chiun knew what Remo was going through with that nine-foot people-crusher, and didn't even have a good word for him afterward. And now the old beanbag was skipping straight into the clutches of a madman who was out to kill them both. Just because the Dutchman kept his elbow straight. Well, fine. If that was how Chiun wanted it, that was just fine with Remo. He would sit in his spot by the sea till flowers bloomed out his ears, and after the Dutchman had sprung his inevitable trap on Chiun, Remo would go up to the white castle to pick up the pieces. Fine. Just fine. Absolutely fine.

With a sigh, he stood up and shambled off toward Devil's Mountain. It didn't matter how Chiun felt about him. He needed Remo, whether he knew it or not, and Remo would be there.

Eleven

Pierre LeFevre drummed his fingers on the antique mahogany arm of the room's lone chair. The starkness of the castle surprised him at first. Each dark chamber he passed through on his way to the Dutchman was as bare and cold as a dungeon, furnished with a dungeon's sparse amenities.

He shifted nervously in his seat, catching the acrid scent of his own fear-soured sweat. Beyond, in a glass-enclosed room visible through a slightly open door, the Dutchman peered through a long white telescope at the shipyard far below. He closed the eyepiece and came into the anteroom where Pierre waited for his reward.

"You were quite right," the Dutchman drawled softly, brushing back his thick blond hair with sensitive hands. "There were two men in the shipyard, although I can't imagine what they were

115

doing there. The trucks don't even have wheels on them, you know." He looked to Pierre to see if he could detect a hint of conspiracy. Did the black man know more than he said? Had the bodies in the truck been found by people other than Remo and Chiun? Had the authorities been notified? But Pierre said nothing and only stared at the carpet. No, the Dutchman decided. He's not with them. He's too scared.

The Dutchman couldn't let him live, of course. He wouldn't tell Pierre that Chiun was, at that moment, climbing alone up Devil's Mountain. He wouldn't reveal that Chiun and Remo had somehow killed all five snakes in the compound. The two of them were cleverer than ever the Master had told the Dutchman. But the old man was alone now. Alone he would do combat with the Dutchman. And alone the old man would die.

The Dutchman held out the scrap of paper on which Pierre had written the address of the villa. "This is where they're staying, you say?"

Pierre tried to speak, but his throat felt as if it were stuffed with cotton. He nodded mutely, his eyes wide and bulging. Lordie, what a mistake. Something was wrong in this place. It was cold here, and too still. It reminded him of old Mr. Potts's mausoleum in the cemetery, where Pierre and his cousin had broken in when they were boys. Cold and stale and motionless, like the Dutchman himself. He was like a ghost, that one, dressed in white and moving and talking, but dead all the same.

Pierre avoided the ice-blue eyes as the Dutchman eased himself languidly toward another door. He walked like a cat, Pierre noticed. Not a sound, not a ripple in the white satin smoking jacket he wore. He gestured with his hands. An olive-skinned servant came in silently carrying a silver tray with a bottle and a glass.

"Sherry, Mr. LeFevre?" the Dutchman asked. "I'm afraid I can't join you, but I'm told it's very good."

"N-n-n-n—" Speech had long since left Pierre.

"No? Very well. I thought it might warm you. After all, it's quite cold outside."

Pierre managed a lopsided grin. Cold? It was eighty-five in the shade.

"Don't you feel it?"

Who was this honky kidding? Good thing the Dutchman wasn't drinking. That boy had to be nuttier than Fabienne's old man was the day he flew off Easter Cliff. Then again, there was a definite chill in the air.

"You're shivering. Would you like a sweater?"

Pierre shook his head emphatically. This nigger cutting out of here like a jet engine, man. He skittered toward the doorway. How he would find his way out of the castle was another story, but . . . Jesus, it was freezing!

"Before you go, I'd like to pay you for your trouble," the Dutchman said. He reached into the pocket of his smoking jacket and pulled out two hundred-dollar bills. Tentatively, Pierre accepted them. He screamed once, and they dropped fluttering to the floor. They were like slabs of ice. The Dutchman cocked his head, amused, as Pierre bolted down the corridors of the castle.

He rubbed the gooseflesh on his arms as he barreled down one dark hallway after another. His breath came in ghostly clouds. He'd seen movies of people breathing in the cold, their breath misty and white, but this was the Caribbean. Nobody was cold here. That was the deal, wasn't it, God? No money, but no icicles either. Oh, Lordie, he should never have stolen the Jeep. He should never have come to the castle. Him what looks on the golden boy of Devil's Mountain . . . Mother, he was going to lose his mind, just like old Soubise. Once he got out of this hellhole, he was going to lock himself up in his room for five days with a gallon of Potts Rum, just to make sure he wouldn't, in his madness, go sailing off to outer space.

Far off, he heard the distant creaking of a door. That had to be the front entrance. He remembered the front door to the castle, two huge, medieval slabs bolted together with iron, overlooking a bridge across the castle's moat.

When he reached it, the door stood open. Pierre gasped at the sight outside. An ice storm was blowing with the strength of a hurricane, the shriveled palm trees bent over at 90-degree angles. Their leaves crackled and slapped together, pointing like the fingers of banshees down Devil's Mountain.

"Oh, Lord, no," Pierre whispered. His eyes

moistened. He felt the tears harden to ice on his skin. He stepped onto the bridge, squatting low against the terrible wind that seemed to come from the castle looming behind him. A gust of hail pulled up the thin fabric of his shirt and lashed at his back like bullets.

Somewhere down there was the Jeep, but the ice storm was too thick to see beyond his nose. Somewhere was . . .

Someone was coming.

He could make out a dim outline against the soupy hail. Whoever it was had spotted him.

"Pierre," the voice called. It sounded oddly cheerful.

"Here! I'm here!" He tried to run forward, but his legs had grown stiff and numb, and he tumbled onto his stomach. Oh, so tired. He tried to push himself up from the ground. His fingers popped at the knuckles. The skin on his hands cracked. The blood froze into brown crystals. "Over here " he rasped. The man was running. He would find him.

Pierre closed his eyes to the wind. He would never open them again.

"Pierre?" Remo said, feeling for a pulse in the black man's neck. There was none. He turned over the body. It was soaked with perspiration. Pierre must have been running for some time in the sweltering afternoon heat. Maybe his heart had given out.

He picked up one of Pierre's hands. The skin had been bleeding, and the knuckles were snapped. Was he tortured? Then he saw the fingernails. That was funny. The skin beneath them was blue.

Blue? He looked over Pierre's corpse again, noticing the dry, cracked skin, the sores around the eyes, the blue flesh beneath the fingernails. It was insane.

It was ninety degrees out here. The palms drooped sullenly from the heat. The wispy grass was dry and patched with brown.

And Pierre LeFevre had frozen to death.

Twelve

Inside the castle, the Dutchman bowed low to his visitor. Chiun returned the bow.

"I am honored with your presence," the young man said. "All my life have I waited to meet you."

"It saddens me to meet you," the old Oriental said. "Your work is most promising. This meeting brings me no joy."

"Why?"

"You know why. I have come to kill you," Chiun said.

"And I was born to kill you, Master of Sinanju."

The two men nodded again to each other, and the Dutchman led Chiun to an airy, well-furnished room bounded on three sides by immense French windows that led to wide balconies where orchids of every color grew. "This is the only comfortable room in the castle," the Dutchman said. "I thought perhaps we could talk for a moment before beginning. I have wanted to ask you many questions over the years." The pale eyes were searching and humble.

"You may ask, but I cannot in a few moments teach you the true way. Not after you have spent a lifetime embracing falsehood," Chiun said simply.

"The Master Nuihc was not false!" The Dutchman rose angrily, his cheeks aflame. "He saved me from disaster."

"So he could lead you into a dark tunnel from which there is no escape, and even more certain disaster."

"That's enough!" In a high corner of the room, a painted lamp exploded into sparkles of glass. Chiun watched it break and splinter, untouched. He looked at the Dutchman.

"You were wise to come alone," the young man said.

"This concerns me and you. Not my son."

The Dutchman's face was dark with fury. "Your son! In the same way that Remo is your son, so was Nuihc a father to me. You destroyed that father."

"He was an evil force that sought only personal gain. Nuihc cared nothing . . ."

There was an agitated knock on the door. Sanchez burst in, gesturing wildly.

"What?" the Dutchman growled. "He is here?"

The mute pointed toward an eastern-facing window. Chiun stepped over to it. On the path below, Remo was climbing up Devil's Mountain.

"No," Chiun called. "Go back, Remo!"

Remo looked up, making no acknowledgment that he had seen Chiun, then continued his march up the hill.

The Dutchman's jaw worked nervously. "He has come to help you," he said, amazed.

"Go away. I don't want you. I told you I was finished with you, white thing."

Remo didn't answer.

"Do not open the gates to him. Send him away," Chiun pleaded. "He has no part in this. Leave him alone."

"He is a true son," the Dutchman said, his voice heavy with sadness. "Clearly you have tried to turn him from you to keep him from danger. But he would die for you. And so he will."

The drawbridge lowered over the fetid, murky green water of the moat. As the enormous oak doors opened, Remo glimpsed a double file of beautiful women standing at attention inside.

"Hello, ladies," he said pleasantly. The girls devoured him with their eyes.

At the end of the line, the mute came forward and led him up a long, curving staircase to the room where Chiun waited with the Dutchman. Remo and the Dutchman stood looking at each other.

"I'm Remo."

"I am Jeremiah Purcell." Neither offered a handshake.

"Why have you come?" Chiun asked in anguish.

Remo looked at the old man for a moment before speaking. "I thought you might need me," he said.

The Dutchman flushed again. "We were just having a chat. Would you care for some tea? I know you don't drink."

Remo started to shake his head, but Chiun said, "I would like some tea."

"Very well." He gestured to Sanchez, who stood by the door, and the mute disappeared. In a few moments he reappeared with a lacquer tray bearing three Korean porcelain cups and a teapot made of red clay. Remo sat down.

"That is from Sinanju," Chiun said, eyeing the teapot.

"It was a gift from my father," the Dutchman answered. He added quietly, "That is, I found it here."

"Was that Nuihc?"

"You seem surprised. Did you think you were the only person in the world to inherit the teachings of Sinanju?"

"Yeah," Remo said. "That's what I was told. I was told a lot of things. But that wasn't what surprised me. You called him Father. Nuihc didn't strike me as the fatherly kind, that's all."

The Dutchman poured the tea and passed the tiny unhandled cups to Remo and Chiun. "He was not, perhaps, the image of a father one would hold. He was a . . . stern man."

Remo and Chiun exchanged glances.

"But he saved me from a life of imprisonment and scrutiny. You see, I am no ordinary assassin."

"No," Remo said, "Nuihc was a baboon, so you're the son of a baboon."

Purcell sipped his tea. At the moment when he lowered his eyes, Chiun hurled his teacup, still full of steaming liquid, toward him. The Dutchman reached up lazily and caught it just in front of his face, careful not to spill a drop.

"As I was saying, I am no ordinary assassin. And not a baboon. You will not defeat me by surprise, Chiun." He handed the cup back to him gently with both hands.

Chiun said calmly, "Apologies for the rudeness."

"Quite all right. I would have done the same myself if I were not certain you would catch the cup."

"This is so sweet," Remo said, "that you're both making me sick."

"How old are you, my son?" Chiun asked the Dutchman. Remo flinched at the words.

"I am twenty-four years old. I was not to do battle with you until my twenty-fifth year, but circumstances . . ." He shrugged.

"You are not ready," Chiun said.

The Dutchman set his teacup down. "I am ready. The Master's will has brought you to me, and I will avenge him."

"Hi ho, Silver," Remo said. "You forget, pal. There are two of us."

The Dutchman smiled. "But you don't count," he said. "I may come to this confrontation a year before my time, but Chiun is many ages past his.

He is a has-been. You, on the other hand, are a never-was."

Remo stood up.

"Stop, stop," Chiun said. "We have no time for insults, and no energy to spare. There is no need for any of us to die sweaty. I wish to know about you, Jeremiah."

Remo walked to the windows and gazed out at the balconies and the terraced lawns below as the Dutchman told Chiun about the farm, his parents, the incident with the pig, the day on the train. Remo agreed enviously that it had been an extraordinary life. Maybe springing full-grown into the training of Sinanju, as Remo had done after years of dissipation, couldn't stand up to the kind of training the Dutchman had had—year after year of strict study since childhood. And Chiun, for all his nagging perfectionism, had allowed Remo to make mistakes. His bent elbow, for one. Nuihc would have allowed no mistakes.

No wonder Chiun thought the Dutchman was such a prize. He was perfect, the prick. Remo began to feel the loose stirrings of self-doubt.

"He sent me to school in Switzerland," the Dutchman was saying. "I was good in languages. At times I thought I might graduate like any other student and work as a translator. I think I might have liked that." For a moment, the icy eyes thawed, remembering a time long gone when hope was still something that belonged to everyone, even the Dutchman.

"And?" Chiun asked.

The eyes retreated behind their glacial façade

126

again. "It was not my destiny," he said. "The school found out about my unusual abilities."

"The exploding lamp?" Chiun asked.

He nodded.

"What about Pierre?" Remo asked from the windows. "He froze to death. In this weather."

"Sometimes it's hard for me to control this . . . this thing." Purcell looked apologetically at the old man. "I won't use it with you, though. We'll fight fairly."

"Let Pierre tell you how fair he is," Remo said.

The Dutchman pretended not to hear. "When the school found out, they put me in a special room with no exits, and they brought in a team of doctors and scientists to poke and probe at me. They never let me rest, always sticking me with needles and trying drugs on me."

"Poor little stinkums," Remo said. "They just wouldn't let you kill people in peace, like all the other homicidal maniacs."

The Dutchman colored deeply, but continued. "After six months, I managed to escape during one of my supervised outings. I ran for the communications office and signaled Nuihc in Lisbon. Two days later he arrived and demolished the place. There's no trace of the school now. Then he brought me here, to train. And wait for you. He hated and feared you, you know. I never saw him again."

Chiun put down his teacup with a silvery tinkle. "I never knew Nuihc had adopted an heir. And why? He held no ties to anyone, as far as I knew."

The Dutchman stooped slightly. "I don't think I

127

was his heir. You see, he never expected to die. But he wanted a partner with my mental abilities. That was why he trained me. In the end, he wasn't able to use me."

"I suppose you know what Nuihc would have done to you once your usefulness got in his way," Remo said.

"You swine!" The Dutchman moved his arm in a sweeping arc. Remo felt a hundred knives come crashing in on his bad leg where the python had crushed it. He buckled, gasping, to the floor.

"You gave your word," Chiun spat, rushing over to Remo.

"To you. To you alone. Not to untrained vermin like him."

"Our talk is finished," the old man said. He cradled Remo's head in his hands.

"I'm all right," Remo said between clenched teeth. "Don't fight him without me."

Chiun whispered softly into Remo's ear. "I must. That was why I left you at the shipyard. He is too much for you. I have trained your body, but his weapon is his mind. He promises not to use his power, but he cannot keep that promise, because Nuihc, in all his teaching, did not teach him right from wrong. We must not allow him to kill us both at once, Remo. If he kills me, then you must fight him. Not before."

"I can't let that happen," Remo groaned.

"I hope I have taught you right from wrong," Chiun said. "Obey me, for the good of us both." He stood.

The Dutchman nodded to Sanchez. The mute

128

helped Remo off the floor and led him, limping, down a long corridor. Remo looked back. Chiun was watching him silently. When Remo was out of sight, Chiun spoke.

"You call Nuihc your father. Did he ever refer to you as his son?"

The Dutchman looked at him sharply. "What gives you the right to ask such a question?"

"As I thought. And so, when I say that Remo is my son and that I love him, does that make you wish to harm him?"

"He is nothing. Nothing compared with me."

"And still no one will call you 'son.'" The hazel eyes shone with pity. "You could have been fine, Jeremiah Purcell. But now you will be dead. Fatherless and dead."

The Dutchman stood stock still, his breathing heavy. Working to keep his face expressionless, he pointed to the four corners of the room. As if commanded, a thick fog inexplicably rolled in from the corners. It covered the floor and curled its way up the walls. "Poison gas," he hissed.

"Nuihc taught you well in his skills of lying and treachery. You cannot keep your word, can you? So important is it that I see your power and your worth." He shook his head sadly.

"I keep my word to kill you," the Dutchman answered. "Come outside and fight, or die here like a coward. Our moment has come, old man." He threw open the French windows and leaped to the balcony, then to the lawn below.

It is illusion, Chiun told himself as the room careened around, the air choking him. The old man crawled out the window to the balcony and balanced on the rail. Below, the terraced gardens tilted crazily, the effects of the Dutchman's conjured poison still thick in Chiun's body. Good, the Oriental said to himself. He has shown me his capabilities. I understand the enemy. Now I can fight him.

Rest, Remo, my son. Your time with him may soon come.

On the railing of the balcony, Chiun drained his lungs of the poison gas and filled them with clean air. He slowed his heartbeat.

The Dutchman waited below, his pale eyes glowing with anticipation and fear. He was going to do combat with the ancient Master of Sinanju. The end was coming, one way or the other. Blessed end to a life no one should have to live.

"I am your destiny, Chiun," the Dutchman said quietly. "Come do battle with the spirit of the dread Master Nuihc."

Chiun stepped off the railing.

Thirteen

Alberto Vittorelli lay unconscious on a cot in the ship's infirmary, covered by an oxygen tent brought by two Dutch island doctors. Dr. Caswell instructed the nurses to watch the makeshift monitors closely as the ship's crew prepared the island's ambulance speedboat for departure.

It was five P.M. Caswell was numb with fatigue. Not since his days as a medic in the Pacific during World War Two had he been called on to treat a patient for shock, third-degree burns, an amputated limb, and massive infection all at the same time. As the two Dutch G.P.'s slapped him wearily on the back in congratulations, he felt a surge of gratitude for the training of those wartime years.

He had been planning to retire in a few months. The cushy cruise ship job was Caswell's last stab at a youth long departed. It hadn't turned the

131

trick for him: age and defeat, he discovered, crept up on him in the middle of the Caribbean as easily as they did anywhere else. But just when he had begun to give in to time, when the ambition and fervor of a young surgeon seemed a thousand years past, Alberto Vittorelli came, burned and mutilated, into his hands. And with those hands Caswell had healed again. Vittorelli was alive.

It had all been worth it, after all.

He stripped off his sweat-soaked surgical gown and stepped outside the infirmary. On deck, the captain paced, his youthful face twisted into a scowl.

"We're finished, Captain," Caswell said. "We'll have him on the speedboat in twenty minutes."

"Nine hours," the captain roared. "Do you realize what this means to my schedule? The passengers can forget Jamaica. We'll have so many reports to fill out, we won't see daylight for six weeks. Your commission is shot, by the way. This kind of delay is inexcusable."

"This kind of delay saved a man's life," the doctor said quietly.

"He'll probably die in the hospital anyway," the captain muttered. He strode away.

Before he knew what he was doing, Caswell heard his own voice shouting, "Just a minute, you pompous ass."

The captain stopped abruptly and whirled around. "*What* did you call me, mister?"

"It's 'Doctor.' I am a doctor, a fine doctor at that, and you are an idiot with sardines for brains. How *dare* you presume that your precious schedules are more important than one breath from Alberto Vittorelli's mangled body? How dare you speak to me of losing a day in Jamaica when in that infirmary a man is alive who would surely be dead if it weren't for nine hours of my work?"

The captain's eyes narrowed. "Why, you ungrateful rum dum! I'll see that you never work another ship again."

"Wonderful!" Caswell laughed merrily. "No more sticking tongue depressors down the throats of lonely old widows. No longer the dispenser of seasickness pills." He looked at his hands. "I am a surgeon, Captain," he said proudly. "I have better things to do before I die than work for you."

"Then you'll do them on that island, you stupid old loon," the captain said, pointing to Sint Maarten. "I'm ordering you off my ship immediately."

"May I say it's the most intelligent order you've ever given. And by the way, Vittorelli won't die in the hospital. I'll be there to make sure he stays alive. Remember me—and men like me—when *you're* dying, Captain." He turned and walked back to his cabin, where a suitcase and a new life waited.

The captain sputtered impotently. Then two women passengers strolled by, nodding and giggling, and the captain resumed his mask of boyish confidence.

He walked briskly to the radio control room. The operator, a swarthy Mediterranean, was eating a salami sandwich. The air in the small room was redolent with garlic. *We've been overrun by guineas,* the captain said to himself, making a note to replace all foreigners on the ship's crew with good Englishmen. Except the cooks. If there'd been a decent meal to be had in Britain, he would never have left for the sea in the first place.

"Radio St. Rose's Hospital," he barked. The radio operator lifted his headset. "Tell them we're bringing in the wounded man. Then prepare for departure."

The operator's eyes widened. "He's alive? Vittorelli's alive?"

"Yes, yes. Send the message. And air out this cabin, in the name of the Queen."

"Yes, sir." When the door closed behind the captain, the radio operator called in the glad tidings. There was a whoop at the other end as the operator at St. Rose's repeated the message to the staff.

"Good work," the St. Rose dispatcher said. "Get our doctors back here."

"Will do," the ship's operator began to say, when a roar of static over the headphones made him jump out of his seat.

"Giuseppe Battiato?" a flat voice asked from the other end of the transmission. The Italian crossed himself. It was like the voice of fate, booming and authoritative, calling him by name from an unknown source.

"Y-y-y-si?" the operator answered.

"This is a scrambled line," the voice said. "No one on this frequency can hear us. Do you still read me?"

O Madre Dio. "I read you."

Fourteen

Remo felt as if he were in a dream, floating. Soft white hands of women caressed him. Eager lips brushed his face. He half focused on the small stone cell with its barred window, where he had been brought, screaming in pain, so long ago.

The pain. His leg no longer hurt him. Funny, the pain had been so bad before. He was sure he'd passed out from it, but now he felt nothing

One of the girls, a voluptuous blonde, found his tongue with hers as she weaved deliciously in front of him. The other girl, a brunette beauty, tackled his belt buckle with deft expertise.

Suddenly there was a loud whooshing of air and a sharp crack. The blonde's smile froze and vanished as she fell backward, a metal dart vibrating in her breastbone. Another thwack, and the brunette slumped dead at Remo's feet.

He shook his head, unbelieving, and turned to look at the tiny prison window behind him. Through the bars, he saw his housekeeper's fat face peering hotly at him, a straw peashooter between her lips.

"Sidonie."

"Get up, fool. The old man need you. Get out of there." She shifted her tremendous bulk in a rustle of skirts and produced a length of iron pipe, which she lowered halfway through the bars.

"You push that way, I push this way. We bend the bars, you get out. Got it?"

"Chiun," he groaned through the fog in his brain. The pipe fell to the floor.

"Pick that up, boy," Sidonie said, irritated. "I walk all the way to de Jeep for that. Now you help me use it to get you out, or I knock your block off with this peashooter, okay? It got poison on de end, so don't try no funny stuff." She puffed her cheeks menacingly.

Forcing himself to alertness, Remo reached up to the bars on the window and pulled them apart with his hands, then hoisted himself through the opening.

"Not bad, white boy," Sidonie said, impressed. "Where Pierre? I still got his money. He come in that?" She pointed to the abandoned Jeep.

"He did. He's dead, Sidonie."

Her mouth turned downward. "That boy have no business coming to Devil's Mountain," she said. She waddled heavily in front of him.

"How'd you get here?"

"I can't keep Fabienne in that house, Mr. Remo.

Not and keep us both alive. They coming for her, the Dutchman's men. We leave, they come. I seen them. It bad, Mr. Remo."

"How'd you know we'd be here?"

She smiled ruefully. "I be in the Resistance, boy. I know you ain't no tourists. The Dutchman, he something funny. He your business here, I figure."

"Where's Fabienne?"

"I hide her out in these caves near here—"

A scream pierced the air. "Dat her!" Sidonie puffed toward the brush. Fabienne screamed again.

"Where is she? I can get there faster alone."

"Over there." She pointed toward a molehill of volcanic pockets sprouting out of the earth beneath a large almond tree. Remo ran to the mouth of the largest cave, which seemed to be connected to the others.

"Fabienne?"

"Remo!" the girl shrieked below. There was a scuffle and another scream, followed by a series of unintelligible grunts. Remo blinked to adjust his eyes to the darkness as he descended deeper into the cave.

In the distance he saw the mute. "Get to the mouth of the cave!" he shouted to the girl. She scurried away.

Deep in the darkness of the cave, Sanchez turned silently to Remo, a knife flashing as he yanked it from between his teeth and raised it above his head to lunge. Remo dodged him and ran even deeper into an obscure channel of the cave. The air was cool and still here. It reminded him of the Dutchman's castle, except that there was no light at all, not even enough to catch the metal of the mute's knifeblade. It was pitch black. Even Remo's trained night vision was worthless.

He reached a hand up experimentally. The ceiling was low. Long stalactites protruded like icicles above him. He tried to find the walls by touch to locate an avenue of escape.

Suddenly the air split as the mute's blade skimmed close by Remo's chest. He backed off involuntarily, breaking off one of the stalactites with a crash. The blade lunged again. By instinct, Remo moved away from the sound a split second before it would have struck him.

Another arc of sound crashed near his left ear. He twisted toward it, bringing his foot up in a ferocious kick. It struck flesh. The mute snarled and brought the knife down over Remo's neck, but it hit only the hard cave earth below. Remo followed the sound of the knife striking and scooped up the mute in both arms. Before the writhing man in his arms could raise his weapon again, Remo thrust him to the ceiling, where a stalactite speared and held him like an insect on a pin.

The mute emitted a low, guttural moan, his arms and legs stirring the dark air briefly, then was silent again. The air returned to stillness.

"Fabienne? It's all right. Say something. It'll lead me to the entrance."

"This way," her voice called from far away, echoing through the empty chambers of the caves.

"Keep talking."

"Over here, Remo." The sound came from a dozen places at once. Over here, over here, over here.

"Never mind. I can't tell where you are." He thought for a moment. "Fabienne, pick up two stones. The bigger the better. Bring them to the dark mouth of the cave, away from the entrance."

After a moment, she spoke. "All right." All right, all right, all right, the walls echoed.

"Now hit the stones together. Put one on the ground if you have to. Just keep hitting."

When his echo died down, he pitched his hearing low. Now he caught the cave's secret sounds: the slow dripping of lime water in the stalactite chambers behind him, the beating of distant bats' wings, soft as night. Silence, Chiun had taught him, was never silent if you listened carefully enough. He fixed his hearing again, to an even more sensitive level.

Now the air he had thought so still whirled and moaned like a desert storm around him. He stepped forward; his shoes squealed. He heard his heart thumping slowly, his blood gushing into his veins. Any sudden loud noise now would have the same effect on him as a syringe full of strycchnine: his nerves would shatter and collapse from the shock. He didn't dare enlarge his hearing further. One level lower, and the sound of his own swallowing would stop his heart.

It was there. Far ahead and to the right: the soft chink of rock on rock. It echoed too, but the hard, metallic sound carried more purely than a human voice. He could trace its source. He followed it slowly, desensitizing his hearing as he inched his way toward the sound.

"Remo?" It was a whisper, but the sound was stunning. He breathed deeply and brought his hearing much closer to the surface.

It was still there. Click. Pause. Click. It sounded further away than ever because Remo's hearing was almost at normal level. He moved quickly toward it.

At last he saw a tiny spark in the distance, repeating with each striking of the stones. A flash . . . another. Soon he could see the outline of the girl lifting the heavy stone.

"You're a doll," Remo said. She wound her arms around him as he led her from the cave to the shade of the almond tree.

"Wait here for me—or Sidonie, if I don't come back," he said.

"Where are you going?"

"I've got to settle some unfinished business."

Fifteen

Giuseppe Battiato, the *Coppelia's* radio operator, was pooling all his spiritual resources to keep from wetting his pants.

Puta, it was the *puta* in Barcelona who did this. He should never have married her. Alberto was right: what business did a father of four have taking a second wife before he'd gotten rid of the first? Live with her in Barcelona, Alberto said. Sample her honey treasure. Life is short. But one wife is enough for any man.

O stupido! He banged himself square in the forehead with his fist. Bigamy was a bad charge. Why hadn't he listened?

"Are you there?" the disembodied voice in his headphones called again. "Repeat, do you read me?"

"I read, I read," Giuseppe answered disgustedly.

"I need some information, Mr. Battiato."

He bet he did. The slut. How did she track him down to the middle of the Atlantic Ocean? He heard his own breath seething between his teeth. The motherless whore. She had probably called up Maria. . . . No, the bitch still didn't know how to use a telephone. She went to see her. God in heaven, the streets of Naples were doubtless running with blood at this moment.

"Are you from the government?" Battiato asked.

"Yes. In a manner of speaking."

He knew it! And then the two bitches had gone together to the *polizia* to demand his arrest. He would never trust a woman again. How they would laugh when he was dragged off to prison! Hah! Giuseppe in shackles. Well, he would tell them both that the cold steel of manacles was more comforting than a woman's treacherous heart, that was for sure.

"The wounded man on your ship, Alberto Vittorelli—"

"No!" Alberto! Could it have been Alberto? Crying fleets of angels, did his best friend sic the authorities on him? He would kill the bastard, the slimy dog dropping; he would cut out his black heart with a burning poker. . . .

"Is there a problem? He's still alive, isn't he?"

"He is alive," Battiato rumbled. But not for long. What was Alberto doing with Francesca in Barcelona? The pig, rutting with his best friend's . . . A thought crashed in on him. What if it

142

wasn't Barcelona? What if it was Naples? His wife. Maria, you cheating bitch!

"I kill him!" he roared.

"I beg your pardon?"

Giuseppe pulled himself together, wiping his face with the back of his hand. "So sorry, *signor*. No problem. What do you want?"

They want my *dick*, that's what they want. The three of them would take his manhood, limp and gray after years of prison, and throw it to the dogs on the street. That is what his mighty weapon is for, they would say. And poor Giuseppe would be at their mercy.

Tears flooded down Battiato's face. "Don't listen to them!" he cried. "They are a pack of filthy liars. On my mother's sainted head, I swear—"

"Mr. Battiato," the flat voice broke in impatiently. "My business is rather urgent. I would appreciate it if you would speak up. There seems to be some difficulty."

"All right," Giuseppe sobbed. "I come into port." He would come in with a knife in his sleeve. He would fight them to the death.

"That won't be necessary. Just stay on the line."

There was a series of electronic poops and squeals. Then the voice said, "Do you read me now?"

"I read you." He would get even. One night, a little ground glass in the manicotti.

"I want you to find out how Mr. Vittorelli was injured."

"What?"

The voice began to repeat. Battiato interrupted it. "You want to know about his *injuries*?"

"That is correct—"

"What about lying with my wife? What about cheating with the *puta* in Barcelona?" he bellowed. "Does that count for nothing?"

"Not at the moment, Mr. Battiato," the voice said, puzzled. "If you don't mind—"

"What am I saying?" He slapped himself twice.

"I'm sure I don't know. Now about Mr. Vittorelli . . ."

"A shark. A shark bit him on the leg. Very bad."

"Before the shark. The electric burns. You did radio in this morning about high-voltage burns, didn't you?"

"Yes . . ." Battiato was sweating profusely. "Who are you?" he asked. Maria had a cousin in Sicily. Money everywhere, the thieving whoremonger.

"My identity is of no consequence."

"Vito! I know it is you, Vito, and they are lying bitches!"

"My name is definitely not Vito," the voice continued calmly. "I want you to find out how Vittorelli got his burns. I know that you are friends with the patient."

Giuseppe eyed the microphone suspiciously. "Why should I?"

"Well, it's a—it's a good thing to do, Mr. Battiato."

Giuseppe laughed. "You want to find out about Alberto just because it's a good thing? Who you jerking off?"

144

The headset sputtered. "You are making a simple request more difficult," the voice said unpleasantly. After a pause, it added, "Very well. There'll be a reward."

"What for? What makes Alberto so special? What for you so interested in the sauce chef?"

"I cannot reveal that, Mr. Battiato."

"Vito, I swear—"

"And I promise you I am not this Vito person," the voice crackled. "Now see here. I have lost all patience with you. I am making a simple request that could save the lives of countless persons. I have offered you a reward for obtaining this harmless information for me. There is no reason on earth why you can't get it, and time is running out. Now, for the love of God, do it."

Giuseppe gasped. O Sainted Mother, could this be a test? Not by Vito, but a test by a greater force? A message like this came once in a lifetime, once in ten thousand lifetimes. Saint Bernadette received such a message. So did Joan of Arc and Francis of Assisi. Maybe their talks with the Almighty didn't occur over a radio transmitter, but God always did work in mysterious ways.

Giuseppe fished out a rosary from his tool kit. He was one of the Chosen, singled out to bring information to Someone very concerned about old Al Vittorelli, who must have said a heap of Ave Marias while he was decurdling the hollandaise.

"But how can I—o, Madonna—" he burst into a stream of rapid Italian.

"Speak English, please. I don't understand any other language," the flat American voice said.

Giuseppe fell backward off his chair. American? After all this time, God was an *American*? All those Paternosters for nothing!

"How can I find out?" Battiato enunciated carefully.

The voice rang with urgency. "Ask him."

"Oh, *si*. I mean yes. I will. I will, you will, he will, we will, they—"

"Stay on this frequency. Radio back when you've got the information. And make it fast, Mr. Battiato. I'm counting on you."

"Yes, sir!" He tore off the headset and threw the door open with a bang. Saint Giuseppe was on the mission of his life. He would find what He—the powerful voice on the supernatural frequency—needed to know. He would, she would, we would, they would . . .

"Vittorelli!" The radio operator burst into the infirmary like a house afire. "Alberto, this is the most important day of our lives! Talk to me." He slapped aside the frantic nurses like flies as Vittorelli struggled to show the whites of his eyes.

"Listen, Alberto," Battiato rumbled in Italian. "You got to tell me how you got burned. Somebody very important wants to know." The nurses had him by both arms.

"Grmpph," said the patient, a line of drool cascading down his chin.

"Wake up, asshole. God is calling for you."

"Oh, no," Vittorelli whimpered. "I am dead."

"No, you're not dead!" Battiato yelled.

"Get his neck. I'm going to pin him into a hammerlock," said one of the sturdy Dutch nurses.

"Quick. Where did you get the shock?"

Vittorelli's watery eyes rolled and fluttered. "The shock? Yes, the electricity."

"That's it," the radio man cheered. "Where did you find the electricity?"

The patient's eyes closed again.

"*Mamma mia*, Alberto, wake up! *Aiii!*"

"Got him," said the nurse. "Over this way, young man." She steered him toward the door.

"Where, Alberto, where?" the radio man shrieked as he was dragged off.

Vittorelli's voice was soft and faraway sounding. "A shipyard. There was a man. . . . Yellow hair and terrible blue eyes . . ."

The door slammed in Battiato's face.

He reeled back to the radio room, stunned, and slipped the earphones over his head. "God?" he said meekly.

"I read you, Battiato. What did you find out?"

"It was at the shipyard, sir. The Soubise shipyard."

"I see."

"Sir, I have been on this island many times, and—and I know the legends and—"

"Yes?"

"Vittorelli says he met a man there, a man with golden hair and eyes of blue. . . ."

There was a pause. Then the voice at the other end answered resolutely, "The Dutchman."

"*Dio*," the operator screamed, falling to his knees. "You know!"

"Yes, I am aware of a few facts," the voice said flatly. "Thank you for your help, Mr. Battiato."

147

"Father, bless me!"

"I beg your pardon?"

"Bless me, Father, for I am your instrument."

"Er . . . very well. Consider it done. Over and out."

A blast of static once again filled the transmission, followed by silence. Giuseppe Battiato remained on his knees, tears of ecstasy flowing down his face.

Sixteen

Ten miles inland, in a shack high on a hill overlooking the Dutch lowlands, Harold W. Smith switched off his radio and removed his earphones. He jotted down a note to send Giuseppe Battiato ten dollars. That was ample reward for the information gathered. Sometimes the simplest operations got to be complicated, he thought with a sigh.

According to his Timex Quartz, it was 5:18:43. Smith loved accuracy.

There were other things he loved: his wife, his stamp collection from his childhood; he loved Vermont, his country, and CURE, of course. But above all he loved accuracy. The idea of life as an ordered, finite course where right and wrong were as different from one another as black and white gave him an indestructible sword with which to fend off the parries of inconsistency. Men were either good or they were disposable; that was just the way things were. It was for this reason that Smith permitted himself a small sigh of relief as he turned to the suitcase-sized computer hookup at his right and keyed in Giuseppe Battiato's information.

Remo was still good. He had suspected from the beginning that Remo didn't commit the murders in the truck body, but words like *suspect, guess, hope,* and *hunch* had no meaning in his vocabulary. His suspicion, when stacked against a dozen murders performed in precisely Remo's style, carried as much weight as a chicken's whistle. Facts were what mattered, and the facts had been against Remo.

But now the facts were shifting their direction. Some quiet probing into the Soubise shipyard had unearthed more information. One, the Soubise yard was by far the most likely source for the truck body found in the ocean. It was the nearest and largest. Not enough to stand up in a court of law, but a fact. Two, the executives of the Soubise enterprise had turned out to be an unorthodox lot, to say the least. They were all drawing fortunes from the shipyard, as were a host of lawyers and brokers around the world. Everyone connected with the business was rich—except for the owner, one Jeremiah Purcell, known locally as the Dutchman, who drew $5,000 a month and whose signature was not affixed to any legal document concerning the shipyard. Moreover, the $5,000 was a cash payment, disbursed at an unknown location.

Three, the only record of Jeremiah Purcell known to mankind—or to Harold W. Smith, who was infinitely more accurate—was a duplicate of a student's registry from a private school in Switzerland. The school had been destroyed in an unexplained explosion in the early '70s. Whoever Purcell was, he kept his comings and goings to himself.

Four, a new batch of disappearances had been reported to the police in Marigot that morning. All of the missing men had been unemployed, all known drunks. There were only five missing-person reports, but the police suspected more than five missing persons. They had spoken of it among themselves at the precinct station Smith had bugged. And Remo wasn't abducting the men. Chiun was watching, waiting for the right moment to kill his pupil. If he'd found Remo killing, the moment would have been at hand.

Two feet of paper filled with printed matter streamed out the top of the computer. At 5:21:04 two more lines responded to Smith's inquiry:

PROBABILITY HIGH CONNECTION VITTOREL-LI/SOUBISE YARD PROBABILITY HIGH CON-NECTION DISAPPEARANCES/PURCELL

He read the lines, tore off the sheet of paper, rolled it into a tube, and burned it. He replaced the computer in one suitcase and the radio in the other and slid them both beneath the floorboards.

He put on his hat. He was not going to waste Remo if he could help it.

* * *

Remo's villa was in ruins. Machine gun fire had gutted the rooms, and fire had scorched the walls. A television set, oddly, was packed into the plaster. Except for that detail, the place had obviously been set up for execution. Someone was after Remo, or Chiun, or both.

Smith made a quick tour of the house. Chiun's trunks were still intact. A black T-shirt lay neatly folded in a bedroom dresser, and a pair of gray chinos hung in the closet. Near the bed, a woman's nightgown lay crumpled on the floor. There was no blood, except for a few stains, which Smith judged to be more than a day old, on the living room carpet.

It occurred to Smith that the two of them might already be long dead.

But if they weren't, he knew where they'd be.

"I need a helicopter," he told the ground crew chief at Juliana airport.

"This is a restricted area, sir," the man barked over his shoulder.

Smith took out his old C.I.A. identification. "This is an emergency. I'll return the vehicle."

The chief spoke rapidly into his headset, and the crewman on the airstrip guided in a KLM 747. "I'd like to help you guys out, mister, but I haven't got an extra pilot."

"That's all right. I'll fly it myself."

The man with the headset took a long look at the middle-aged fellow whose I.D. claimed he was Dr. Harold W. Smith, computer information specialist. He was wearing a three-piece gray suit, a straw hat, and glasses. All in all, he wasn't the chief's idea of an ace pilot.

"How many hours you got logged?" he asked.

"Seven thousand. I'll bring it back within a half-hour. You can keep my card."

The ground control chief flipped the card over in his hand. "Well, okay, if it's an emergency. But if that machine isn't back here in time, I'm going to put out an area search for you, including airspace."

"That's fine. Thank you very much."

"In the west hangar." He watched Smith trot off. They sure aren't very fussy about their agents down in Langley these days, he thought.

Then, just as Smith got the chopper off the ground, the air to the northwest lit up in a soaring explosion of flame.

Smith knew his suspicions had been right.

Seventeen

Chiun's blue ceremonial robe lay folded near a cluster of bouganvillea. The Dutchman's white jacket was strewn carelessly over the balcony railing, where he had tossed it. He wouldn't need it after today. He wouldn't need anything.

It was as it should be, he thought. His life was scheduled to begin after his twenty-fifth year; he would never see it. The Dutchman would instead be claimed by the sea, his freakish spirit drowned for all eternity. There would be no more death urged on by the hungry, senseless thing inside him, no more pain. A long swim out, one struggling gasp, and done. After Chiun's death, his own would come easily. An hour had passed since the two men first faced each other in their fighting gis. Although their movements were constant and spectacular, no blow had been struck. Each was aware of the other's lethalness: one blow was all it would take. The slowness of the battle was agonizing. The Dutchman's body was bathed in sweat.

He jumped high in the air, twisting into a perfect triple spiral that jolted his downward spin to incredible speed. The air behind him sparked. He landed less than an inch away from Chiun. His arm was ready, rocketing in the direction of the old man, but Chiun was already fifty feet away, transported as if by sheer magic.

"Excellent," the old man said. "A beautiful variation. But you waste too much energy in unecessary movement. Prepare your feet before you begin the upward thrust. It should help the angle of your landing."

The Dutchman bristled, his concentration broken. "We are met here in mortal combat," he reminded Chiun with the consummate dignity of youth.

Chiun smiled. "I cannot help it. I am too much the teacher."

"I will kill you."

He shrugged. "Perhaps. What will you do then, Jeremiah?"

The Dutchman's jaw worked. "None of your business," he said finally.

"You need not hate me to kill me, you know." The old man's eyes were smiling.

"You murdered Nuihc!" he shouted.

"He murdered himself through his evil. What will you do, my son?"

"Don't call me that!"

"What will you do when I am dead?"

The words rushed out in a torrent of fury. "I will die! I will go to the sea and end the useless pain of my life. I will find rest." Tears streamed over his face.

Chiun stammered. "You will die?"

"That is all I wish."

"But you are so young—"

"I am an abnormality. A cancer. *I set my own parents on fire!*"

"That is done, just as Nuihc's life is done. You cannot change that. But you can control your power. It need not be destructive."

"I can't control it. It only gets worse with each year. Soon I will be killing children on the street. Don't you see? I cannot live. I am an evil thing, not a man. I must not live."

Chiun was puzzled. "Then why do you bother to kill me?"

He answered with downcast eyes. "I have made my pledge to Nuihc."

Night was falling. Beyond the terraced lawns of the castle, the tide rushed inward. The tree frogs of twilight began their eerie song. Chiun walked toward the Dutchman slowly. He stopped in front of him.

"Then kill me," Chiun said simply.

"No!" The young man was enraged. "You are a *legend*. You will fight me. I will not butcher the Master of Sinanju like a defenseless cat." He stepped back. Chiun smiled. "Stop it!"

"I see now," Chiun said. "You did not plan to kill me at all. You wished only that I would kill you."

"That's not true! I promised Nuihc!"

"You are not an evil man, Jeremiah."

"Get away—"

Both men froze in their tracks, their eyes riveted to the silhouette coming over the horizon. Remo stopped, too, looking in bewilderment at the two of them.

"Now I will force you to fight me," the Dutchman said.

The air crackled with electricity. The tree frogs abruptly stopped their song. All was silence.

He raised his right arm slowly. Starting on his shoulder, a ball of light traveled down his arm, growing, glowing brighter, and shot off his finger like a bullet. It hit Remo in the stomach. Remo blinked, stunned, and doubled over with a gasp.

"Halt!" Chiun shouted.

Remo wobbled to his feet. "I think I've just about had it with you," he said.

The Dutchman sent out a wall of air to knock Remo off his feet. At the same time he sent another, stronger one toward Chiun. The old man squinted against the gale, unable to move. The Dutchman closed in on Remo.

Remo rolled out of the way of the first blow, a kick that left a deep pit in the ground. The dirt from the pit swirled and dissipated in the growing windstorm that the Dutchman had created. He struck again. Remo dodged it by instinct alone. The experience in the cave had taught him not to rely on his eyes.

A long tongue of flame licked out of the turbulence. Without thinking, Remo lunged toward it, two fingers poised to strike. They hit. Out of the flying dirt and thick salt spray came a howl. Then the Dutchman's fingernails thrust past Remo's face, near enough to scrape four bloody lines across his skin.

It was hard to breathe in the maelstrom of whirling leaves and earth. Two trees were uprooted nearby. Their gray trunks flew overhead, weightless. Remo lunged again and missed. An invisible foot caught him on the thigh, sending him sprawling through the mist. He kept going when he landed, sure the Dutchman would have heard his fall. The shape came—how fast could that guy move? Remo positioned himself for attack. When the Dutchman touched ground, Remo stepped forward with a thrust to the neck.

He hit. Not the neck. A shoulder groaned in its socket, shattered, and fell away from his fist. Without a second's hesitation, the Dutchman's other arm lashed out and took Remo in the ribs. Two sharp snaps sent Remo back, reeling. An inch closer, and they would have pierced his heart.

Then another shape loomed nearby. Instinctively, Remo charged for it before realizing it was Chiun. He stopped cold as Chiun spoke.

"Move!" the old man said. But Remo moved too late. Chiun's tiny figure in the mist upended and seemed to blow away in the wind.

"Chiun!" Remo called.

Silence.

"Chiun!"

The hand came out of nowhere toward Remo's temple.

"Chiun," he whispered as the walls of consciousness came crashing in blackness around him. It had been a glancing blow, but enough to stop Remo. Enough to weaken him. The next would kill him. He was beaten. It was over. He tasted the dirt on his lips.

And then from the depths of his soul, his voice spoke. "I am created Shiva, the Destroyed; death, the shatterer of worlds. The dead night tiger made whole by the Master of Sinanju."

And he struggled to his feet.

He moved, infinitely slowly, the blood of ages stirring within him. The Dutchman emerged from the storm. His mangled shoulder was dripping blood, and blood was pouring from his side. His face was twisted in pain and rage as he came for Remo.

Silently, swiftly, Remo sprang from his back, his being focused in his powerful right arm. A look of terror flashed across the Dutchman's eyes as Remo struck, tearing his face to a pulpy mass.

At the instant it was over, Remo felt a wave of pity rise in his throat.

The Dutchman staggered off his feet and disappeared backward into the storm. In the mist a fluttering sigh began and died.

Soon the soughing of the wind ebbed. The dead leaves that had been coloring the sky black settled to the ground, and twilight returned in its electric blueness. Far away, a tree frog began singing, and others took up the chant.

"Chiun?" Remo called.

The old man stood near a broken Ackee tree.

Slowly he raised his arm to point toward the cliff side of Devil's Mountain. Across a jagged boulder was draped the broken body of the Dutchman. Remo and Chiun went toward him.

The explosion happened before they reached him. The earth shook, and a double blast burst from the castle in a curtain of flame. Fire poured out of its narrow slit windows. Women screamed.

A second explosion rocked the castle to its foundations. Huge slabs of stone tumbled to the ground as the white turrets crumbled, leaving clouds of dust and fire in their wake.

Chiun took hold of Remo's arm, his long fingernails digging into his skin. "Listen," he said, drawing Remo toward the Dutchman.

The young man's eyes were open and weeping, tears mixed with blood dropping red onto the rock where he lay as Nuihc's castle disintegrated before him. "I have failed," he croaked. "Nuihc, this is your vengeance." Then his head dropped. He made no other movement. Thin streams of blood coursed from his wounds down the gray stone, forming small pools around him. On the peak, the fire raged unabated, washing the Dutchman's body in a bright glow.

"How young he is," Chiun whispered. He picked up his robe and dabbed at the cuts on Remo's cheek. "Come. We must look after you now."

Then, in the orange aura from the blaze in the castle, they saw a line of figures marching toward them, their outlines wavy and rippled in the heat. At the head of the line lumbered a wide female figure who shouted commands at the others.

"*Buge-toi, putain*! Move it. You best be putting them buns to work getting you down this hill, else they gonna burn like de pork rind. Ha, ha," Sidonie cackled gleefully as she forced her charges down the hill.

Chiun peered at the strange parade. All of the figures were women in various stages of undress. Some were draped in sheets or towels; others picked their way down the hill clad only in diaphanous nightgowns. One of them, a proud red-headed Amazon, strutted apart from the group wearing a black garter belt, opera hose, and spike heels.

"That woman in front," Chiun began, pointing to the black drill sergeant in a ruffled skirt and bandana. "She looks like . . ."

"Who else," Remo finished, watching Sidonie wield the iron pipe she had brought to Remo's rescue earlier. She circled it over her head, threatening the girls behind her as she commanded them downward.

"Hey, Mr. Remo, Mr. Chiun," she bellowed. "Lookee what I got for you. Get going, girlie. You ain't laying around sucking up bonbons no more." Behind her, the girls grumbled and muttered in French. "*Taisez-vous*!" she shrieked, prodding one of the girls in the stomach with the pipe. "*Soyez tranquille*! Shut your mouth or I shut it good, hear?"

In silence the girls fell in near Remo and Chiun. From the rear of the line, a little terrier scrambled forward, stopping to beg at Sidonie's feet.

"Who are those people?" Chiun asked.

Sidonie picked up the dog and slung him onto her shoulder. "They the Dutchman's women," she said. "Sinners, all of them. Prob'ly pretty good at it, too, by the looks of them," she added with a wink. "I take them out of the castle after I sabotage the furnace."

"You what?" Remo asked, looking up at the flaming ruin on the hill.

"I take the gasoline tank what was in the Jeep Pierre stole. I drag it into the basement, I throw it in the furnace. Boom."

"*You* made the boom," Chiun acknowledged.

"Bomb," said Remo.

"I be in the French Resistance, remember?"

"And the Dutchman thought it was Nuihc's vengeance," Remo said.

Fabienne and another woman, who was strangely swathed in veils of sooty white gauze, came limping from the direction of the castle. "Remo, Remo!" Fabienne called, waving wildly. Her dirt-streaked face was happier than Remo had ever seen it as she jumped into his arms, sending shooting pains from Remo's fractured ribs.

"It's all right," Remo said over her loud apologies. "It's only my chest."

The woman in white reached over with a visible effort and took the dog Sidonie held out to her. The terrier whined and tried to lick the woman's scarred face beneath her veil.

"Adrianna will testify that the Dutchman used some kind of—how you say—hypno—hypno—"

"Hypnosis."

"Yes. He hurt many people, Remo." She took

the hand of the veiled Asian girl. "Adrianna was nearly blinded. She thinks also that the Dutchman killed people in the shipyard. Perhaps if the police investigate—"

"They will. And they'll find plenty of bodies. You won't have any trouble getting your father's business back. You're rich, Fabienne."

She kissed him, but a shadow of worry passed over her face. "Will the Dutchman go to prison on Sint Maarten? You know, he's very clever. He may escape."

"He's not going anywhere, Fabienne." He turned toward the jagged rock where the Dutchman had fallen. "He's d—"

The blood-spattered rock was bare.

Eighteen

He was crawling, wounded and bleeding, down the cliff side of Devil's Mountain, heading for a cluster of fishing boats below. His blond hair bobbed in the twilight as the Dutchman struggled to free a small dinghy while holding his smashed shoulder in place.

"Take these persons to the police," Chiun told Sidonie. "But do not mention Remo or me."

"I get it," Sidonie said. "I knew you wasn't no tourists." Yelling happily, she bullied the girls toward the road leading to Marigot.

The Dutchman wobbled in the small boat. With his good arm, he pulled out the throttle to start the outboard motor. It coughed twice, then purred.

Remo touched his broken ribs. They wouldn't stand up to a descent down a cliff. There was only one way to catch the Dutchman, and that would have to be done perfectly or not at all. "What the hell," Remo said out loud. He'd done it perfectly twenty-four times in a row. He might as well press his luck. He stepped back a few paces and ran off the cliff to begin the Flying Wall. Arms outstretched, he soared over the Dutchman's dinghy, shifting his weight to land alongside it. Painless, he thought as he skimmed on top of the water like a sea bird. The Dutchman watched him with grim resignation.

The boat circled crazily when Remo grabbed hold of it, still traveling fast from the momentum of his dive.

"Just felt like dropping in," Remo said.

The Dutchman stomped on his fingers.

"Is that any way to treat the guy who thought he killed you?"

"Go back to shore," the Dutchman said.

"Sorry, kid. There's a nice girl on the island who doesn't want you running around loose. Not to mention a truckload of dead men who aren't that crazy about you, either."

The Dutchman kicked hard at Remo's head. When he moved out of the way, the Dutchman shoved the throttle up full and sped away. Remo caught up to the boat in two strokes, dove, and caught hold of the outboard's whirling propeller with his hands. Underwater, he heard the motor clink and die.

"Looks like you're staying," Remo said, tossing the propeller into the boat with a clang.

For a moment the Dutchman looked at him

with disgust, but his attention was drawn further out to sea. Two deep lines settled between his eyes as he held out his hand to Remo.

"What? So friendly? I thought you were the last of the bluebloods. No handshakes with the proles."

"Get in," he said urgently.

A gray fin followed in Remo's wake as the Dutchman pulled him aboard. Remo did an unconscious doubletake when he saw the shark's form passing near the boat.

"Guess I owe you one."

The Dutchman stood glaring at him, his hand clutching the red-stained clothing over his shoulder.

"So I'll tell you something. Nuihc's spirit didn't blow up your castle. My housekeeper did. She practices on explosives between dusting and ironing."

The young man said nothing, but his eyes registered a disbelieving relief.

"It's true. Nobody's going to hurt you now. Except for me, that is. Or Chiun. Or the cops." He smiled, but the Dutchman only looked at him silently, his eyes shining and alert with fever.

"You helped me out. I wish you'd tell me why," Remo said.

The Dutchman spoke quietly. "That is not an honorable way for an assassin to die."

Remo grimaced. "You sure don't make it easy to kill you."

"Perhaps I'll kill you first." The blood from his shoulder was streaming through the Dutchman's fingers. His knuckles were pressed hard into the flesh, and his hand was trembling.

"You're hurt."

The Dutchman shrugged.

"Look, Chiun'll never let me hear the end of this, but if you let me take you in to the police station, we'll leave it at that. After you get that shoulder treated, you can break out of any jail they put you in. Just give me your word that you'll leave Chiun and me and the girl alone. And my housekeeper too. Deal?"

"I broke my word to you before."

"I never was a very good businessman, but I'd trust you."

The Dutchman's eyes glistened. "You are a fool. Like the old man."

"I guess there are worse things."

He breathed deeply. For a moment their eyes locked. Then the Dutchman straightened, his quiet arrogance reasserted.

"I have made my promise to Nuihc. You and Chiun must die by my hand." Slowly he moved toward Remo in the rocking boat.

"Sorry to hear it," Remo said.

The Dutchman lashed out an elbow and a knee. The elbow caught Remo in his broken ribs, the knee in his hurt leg. Remo tumbled backward, making the dinghy roll wildly and half fill with water. He kicked out with his legs, rolling off his back. He landed in a crouch, his arms free to launch two fists into the Dutchman's belly. The wind whooshed out of the man.

The Dutchman lunged for Remo, his eyes blinking away the river of blood that filled them. Remo twisted out of the way, dangerously unbalancing the boat. The Dutchman tottered on the edge for a second, his arms windmilling, then fell head first into the sea. He emerged a few feet away from the boat, blood spurting from the bridge of his nose. Nearby, a familiar gray fin hovered uncertainly.

"Quick, give me your hand," Remo shouted. The Dutchman made no move. "It's the shark. He's back. Hurry up."

The Dutchman smiled slowly. "No, thank you, my friend," he said.

"For Christ sake, I'll finish you in the boat if you want. Don't get torn up by a shark."

"It doesn't matter," the Dutchman said, his voice eerily calm. "Please give my regards to your esteemed father."

"Father? I'm an orphan. Get in here, Purcell."

"Your true father. The Master of Sinanju. He has trained you well, in your heart as well as your body. He is right to be proud of you."

He was swimming away awkwardly, a stream of blood behind him. The fin in the distance wavered as the shark smelled prey, then homed in quickly toward the blond head receding in the water.

"Purcell."

"Till we meet in a better life," the Dutchman said.

Then the water churned and bubbled as the fin dipped beneath the surface. Other gray forms slid past the small boat to the frenzied activity in the

168

sea. A pool of red spread through the darkening water. The fins disappeared. The sea quieted. The last rays of sun sank away.

The Dutchman was gone.

Nineteen

Remo stood alone in the small boat, ankle deep in water, enveloped by darkness. High on the cliff he could make out Chiun's outline, still and silent as the sea. He felt tired and pained and lonely.

Out of sight, the distant whirring of a helicopter grew louder. Then the machine appeared over the horizon, sending a searchlight out over the cliff. The light traveled the expanse of the castle, now a smoking wreckage licked occasionally by dying flames, then settled on Chiun. The old man shielded his eyes from the glare and pointed out to sea.

Remo waited unmoving in the boat as the helicopter's searchlight spanned the coral reefs and black night water of the ocean before it reached him. When the helicopter was overhead, a rope ladder dropped from its belly, and Remo climbed onto it. Halfway up, he spotted the sour lemon face of the pilot.

"Come here to see if I'm still alive?" Remo shouted above the noise of the propeller, and climbed up the rest of the way.

Smith turned the helicopter around without a word. The moon had risen, and in its light Smith's sallow face glowed a ghostly greenish white.

"Great tan you got there on Saba with your wife."

"It was a matter of national security," Smith said, as though that vindicated his order to have Remo annihilated.

"National security? What about my security?" Remo yelled. "You order my teacher to murder me because you found a couple of stray bodies, and all you have to say is 'national security'? Well, Chiun's not going to do it. If you want to have me offed, you're going to have to fight me yourself."

"For a time, all the evidence pointed to you."

"For your information, someone else killed those guys in the truck or whatever you found in the ocean."

"I know. Jeremiah Purcell," Smith said.

"His name's Jeremiah—what?"

"I know. It all came out in the wash. Glad the whole thing didn't go further than it did."

The helicopter hovered over the cliff for a moment, then drifted down.

"You've got some gall," Remo grumbled as Smith killed the engine. Chiun walked over and bowed politely. Remo and Smith stepped out.

"Where is he?" Smith asked.

"Who?"

"Purcell."

"You're a little late for him," Remo said. "A half-dozen sharks beat you to him."

"Oh."

"There's plenty of evidence against him. He had another truckload on ice at the shipyard, and a harem full of French hookers are on their way to the police to spill the whole story."

"It is so," Chiun agreed.

Smith grew even paler. "You mean the police are going to be notified about your part in all this?"

"Relax. Nobody even knows we're here."

"The housekeeper does," Smith said quietly.

No one spoke for a long moment. Finally it was Smith who broke the silence. "We can't have witnesses," he said.

"She's not going to talk, Smitty," Remo insisted.

"You can't be sure of that. Also, I've run a check on the Soubise girl."

"Oh, no you don't. Uh-uh. As far as she's concerned, Chiun and I are just a couple of happy sun bunnies. I'm not going to kill Fabienne now that things are finally looking up for her. No way."

"She was spotted leaving your place with the housekeeper. She knows your name."

"That's a lousy reason, Smitty."

"It's national security."

"That's a lousy reason, too."

"I'm afraid I have to order you to eliminate them."

"Yeah? Well, you can shove your orders—"

Chiun put a restraining hand on Remo's arm. "Silence," he said.

Smith was looking up at the smoldering castle. "I'll radio in a call to the fire department," he said. "Meanwhile, the two of you had better go back to the villa and collect your things. You're leaving in the morning. Pick up your tickets by eight at the American counter."

As he was walking back to the helicopter, he said over his shoulder, "Don't be surprised at the condition of your house. It's been ransacked. Some idiot even threw the television through the wall."

"Some idiot," Remo muttered. Chiun elbowed him in the ribs. "Hey," he called, "what about the rest of our vacation?"

"This vacation is over," Smith said flatly. "You'll have to wait until next year. Don't forget to take care of those two women before you leave."

The helicopter roared to life, lifted up, and disappeared.

"He's got the heart of a cod," Remo said.

Chiun wasn't listening. He was staring out at the ocean, a rippling film of black streaked with the moon's lone white ray. "I shall mourn our strange young Dutchman," he said.

Remo felt a knot in his stomach as he recalled Purcell's last words as the sharks closed in on him, bidding Remo to meet him in a better life. "Hell of a way to go."

"If Nuihc had only . . ." Chiun's voice trailed off.

Remo put his arm around the old man. "Let's go, Little Father."

They walked together down Devil's Mountain. Beyond the cliff, the ocean slapped peacefully against the shore. Chiun looked back once, saw nothing, then turned away.

Twenty

Chiun's seven lacquer trunks were stacked in front of the destroyed villa. Remo was inside, changing into his spare set of clothes. His other garments were stuffed into the wastepaper basket.

Chiun came into Remo's room and stood inside the door, his face stony. "You promised you would get me another television," he said icily.

"I didn't exactly have the time, Chiun." He winced as he pulled his T-shirt over his taped ribs.

"If you had kept your promise, I could have been watching television now."

"The taxi's coming in five minutes."

"Five minutes," Chiun mocked. "You act as if five minutes were nothing. Whole empires have collapsed in less than five minutes. Mountains have been leveled. Geniuses are conceived in less than five minutes."

"Only if their parents are into quickies," Remo said.

"You are disgusting!" Chiun shrieked.

"He sure is," Sidonie's voice boomed from the hallway. "Dis place even more of a mess than before. Lookit this." She fished Remo's shirt out of the wastebasket. "How I supposed to wash your clothes what's in the trash?"

"Throw it out, Sidonie. We're leaving."

"Already? Why you want to go so soon?"

"Business," Remo said. "Sorry you had to make the trip over. I couldn't reach you on the phone."

"Oh, I ain't been home. De police, they keep me at the station all night, eating de doughnuts and drinking de rum. They nice fellas. One of 'em got his horns out for Sidonie, too."

"Yeah?" Remo smiled.

"He plenty fat," Sidonie said.

"That's good. I guess. Uh—you didn't mention anything about—"

"I don't say nothing, Mr. Remo. I know you like them secrets. I just tell the police I done it all myself. Fight the Dutchman in the boat, everything. The fat one, he like that plenty," she chortled.

"How about the girls?"

"I tell them if they talk, I kill them dead. They don't say nothing. Except the Chinee girl. She laying it on good about the Dutchman. 'He a killer,' she say. 'He a maniac.' The cops, they have to shoot her fulla dope just to quiet her down."

"And Fabienne—is she okay?"

"Why don't you ask her yourself?" She jerked

her head toward the kitchen. Fabienne stepped forward, her face breaking into a big smile.

"I just wanted to tell you that everything's going to be all right," she said. "The police are already arresting some of the shipyard executives. My lawyer says I'll probably get my father's money back and the company, too."

"Hey, that's terrific," Remo said. "What are you going to do with the shipyard? Sell it?"

"I'm going to run it," she said. "My father would have wanted that." She touched his shoulder. "Of course, you could help me if you like."

Remo kissed her gently. "Thanks, Fabienne, but I'm a bust at office work. You'll do just fine on your own."

"Remo . . ." Her eyes were searching his face. "What do you do? For a living, I mean?"

Chiun cleared his throat. "I see the taxi," he said. Outside, a black London-style cab honked and skidded to an abrupt halt.

"He a salesman," Sidonie filled in.

"But on the cliff that night. And in the cave. You killed—"

."Oh, salesmen very handy guys to have around," Sidonie shouted over her.

Fabienne looked out the window. The cab driver was loading Chiun's trunks onto the roof of the cab. "Are—are you leaving?" she asked.

Remo inclined his head once, sadly.

They stared at each other for a moment. Then Fabienne kissed him softly on the cheek. "I'll miss you," she said.

"Yeah."

"He be back, little darlin'," Sidonie said, clapping a pudgy hand on Fabienne's back. "Ain't that right, Remo?"

"Sure. Why not?" he said, but his words didn't ring true. Smith would never send him back to Sint Maarten. It would be too risky.

"No, you will not return," Fabienne said kindly, sensing his false optimism. "But it is just as well. Later it would not be the same. I will make a new life for myself here. You too, wherever you go. We will be different people, with different dreams. But I loved you, Remo."

He smiled. "You know, you only look like a French pastry," he said, rumpling her hair.

"Remo, the taxi," Chiun called from outside.

"Well, I guess this is it," Remo said. "No more Dutchman, no more Remo."

"I don't know about that," Sidonie said cryptically.

"Huh?"

"Come with me. I think maybe you want to see this."

"But the taxi—"

"Dat Jacques. You give him fifty cent, he wait a week."

Jacques was back in the taxi, drumming on the horn in a lively reggae rhythm. Remo walked over, handed him a hundred-dollar bill, and asked him to wait. Chiun followed him back through the villa, shouting.

"What have you forgotten now? When Emperor

Smith asks why we have missed the airplane, do not expect me to come to your defense."

"Sidonie wants us to see something."

Ahead, the two women walked side by side toward the sea. Remo took pleasure in the sight of Fabienne's auburn hair blown to the side by the breeze, like a shiny copper flag. In the sunlight, the slim outline of her legs showed through the fabric of her skirt.

Suddenly she stopped short, emitted a small cry of shock, and covered her face with her hands. Sidonie's black arm wound around the girl's shoulders.

"What is it?" Remo called, running toward them. The sight on the beach made him stop dead.

By the shoreline, the remains of a giant mako shark littered the sand with bloodied entrails. Fifty feet away, another shark lay dead, its massive jaw gleaming in the sunlight. Its belly was torn open in the same manner as that of the first.

"Lookee that way." Sidonie pointed south, where a lump of gray skin and red flesh washed in and out with the waves. "They be two more thataway, 'round the trees," she said, gesturing in the opposite direction.

The four of them stood in silence as the waves washed over the two massive bodies in front of them.

"He couldn't have done this," Remo whispered.

Chiun was the only one who heard him. "And why not?" the old man said archly, a twinkle reappearing in his hazel eyes.

"He was hurt. Bad. And look at the size of these mothers."

"What you two yakking about?" Sidonie shouted.

Fabienne began to cry. "It's him, isn't it? The Dutchman's still alive!" She was shuddering uncontrollably. Remo put his arms around her and held her tightly.

"He's not alive," he cooed, sounding exactly like the unconvincing liar he was. "He won't be back, I know it."

"Get back, Mr. Remo." Sidonie shoved him aside and, drawing back her dark, calloused hand, smacked Fabienne roundly across the face. The girl started, her tears drying instantly with the impact.

"Now you listen to Sidonie, girl," she bullied, wagging a finger at Fabienne. "I been living a long time, and I seen trouble's face many time. You seen it once, too, but just 'cause it gone now, you think it never going to come back. You wrong, girl. De trouble always 'round the bend. It sit sometime. It wait. But it come back. Right, Mr. Chiun?"

Chiun smiled. "Always."

"But it go away, too. De trouble like the tide. It don't leave for long, but it don't stay long, neither. So if the Dutchman come back one day—" She shrugged. "Dat just the tide coming in again. It be going out before long. You remember that, maybe you get to be as old as me."

She squeezed the girl in her broad arms. Fabienne dried off her face, embarrassed. "You're right," she said. "I am a fool."

"No. You just young." She took Fabienne by one hand and Chiun by the other and led them back to the house. In the taxi out front, Jacques was working himself into a lather, drumming on the steering wheel and howling Bob Marley tunes.

"You try to get back here sometime, Mr. Remo, honey," the housekeeper said, giving his cheek a pinch. "You too, Mr. Chiun."

They waved out the cab window at the two women, who were standing together clutching handkerchiefs. Without missing a beat, Jacques started the engine and shot down the dirt road at eighty miles an hour, plastering Remo and Chiun against the seat.

"He's got to be dead," Remo said.

Chiun sighed. "When will you learn? A shark is only a fish. But Sinanju is Sinanju."

"He was wounded, damn it."

"He was brave."

They rode in silence for a few minutes. "Do you think we'll see him again?"

Chiun was staring out the window. "If we do, he will try to kill us."

"I suppose so," Remo said. "The bastard."

Chiun turned away from the window. His eyes looked directly into Remo's. "My son," he began. "Last evening in the boat, you could have killed the Dutchman. Why didn't you?"

"Why didn't you? You were supposed to be fighting him."

"It is not polite to answer a question with a question. Why didn't you kill him in the boat?"

Remo looked at his hands. "I don't know," he said. "Funny. I didn't even like him. I was jealous, I guess. But it just didn't seem right."

"You know, of course, that Emperor Smith will blame you for any of the Dutchman's killings in the future."

"Yeah, I know."

"You are also aware that Smith will be angry that you neglected to kill Fabienne and Sidonie."

"Did I?" Remo snapped his fingers. "Damn, I knew I forgot something."

The taxi pulled into Juliana Airport. Inside, the place was teeming with pasty-skinned tourists sweating in winter parkas while the ineffective ceiling fans twirled lazily around the flies and mosquitoes.

Remo picked up their tickets, and they filed past the departure gate, the island air outside sweeter and warmer and more beckoning than ever. On the aluminum stairs leading into the plane, Chiun waved at the grumbling crowd waiting behind him.

"I know why you could not kill the Dutchman," he said, smiling happily.

"Why?"

"Do you remember in the Dutchman's castle, when I said I hoped I'd taught you the difference between right and wrong?"

Remo stroked his chin thoughtfully. "Did you say that?"

"Of course I did," Chiun said, his smile vanishing. "Can't you even remember the words of your wise, self-sacrificing teacher?"

Remo sniffed. "Yeah, I guess I did the right thing after all. Old Remo comes through again."

"You are an arrogant lout," Chiun sputtered.

"Just good old American know-how, I reckon." He clapped a hand on Chiun's shoulder.

"Unhand me, ungrateful wretch," Chiun shrieked, creating a buzz in the crowd behind them. "How dare you take the credit, after all my years of toil and hardship . . ."

"I know just how it is," a white-haired woman on the stairs said, poking her face between the two of them. "My son. A doctor. Do you think he can spare five minutes to write to his mother?" She looked at Remo in disgust and turned back to Chiun, clucking sympathetically. "They're all the same."

Chiun's face brightened. "You understand?"

"Oy, do I understand," she said, her eyes rolling heavenward. "The minute my Melvin was born, my heart started breaking."

"Hey, get in the plane," someone yelled behind them. The woman silenced the complainer with her handbag.

"Excellent form," Chiun said. The woman blushed. "Would you care to chat with me during the flight?" he asked. "I'm sure my son will be pleased to ride in the lavatory."

"It's the least he can do," she said, smiling as she elbowed them both past Remo.

CELEBRATING 10 YEARS IN PRINT
AND OVER 20 MILLION COPIES SOLD!

☐ 41-216-9 Created, The Destroyer #1	$1.95
☐ 41-217-7 Death Check #2	$1.95
☐ 40-879-X Chinese Puzzle #3	$1.75
☐ 40-880-3 Mafia Fix #4	$1.75
☐ 41-220-7 Dr. Quake #5	$1.95
☐ 40-882-X Death Therapy #6	$1.75
☐ 41-222-3 Union Bust #7	$1.95
☐ 40-884-6 Summit Chase #8	$1.75
☐ 41-224-X Murder's Shield #9	$1.95
☐ 40-284-8 Terror Squad #10	$1.50
☐ 41-226-6 Kill Or Cure #11	$1.95
☐ 41-227-4 Slave Safari #12	$1.95
☐ 41-228-2 Acid Rock #13	$1.95
☐ 40-890-0 Judgment Day #14	$1.75
☐ 40-289-9 Murder Ward #15	$1.50
☐ 40-290-2 Oil Slick #16	$1.50
☐ 41-232-0 Last War Dance #17	$1.95
☐ 40-894-3 Funny Money #18	$1.75
☐ 40-895-1 Holy Terror #19	$1.75
☐ 41-235-5 Assassins Play-Off #20	$1.95
☐ 41-236-3 Deadly Seeds #21	$1.95
☐ 40-898-6 Brain Drain #22	$1.75
☐ 41-238-X Child's Play #23	$1.95

☐ 41-239-8 King's Curse #24	$1.95
☐ 40-901-X Sweet Dreams #25	$1.75
☐ 40-902-3 In Enemy Hands #26	$1.75
☐ 41-242-8 Last Temple #27	$1.95
☐ 41-243-6 Ship of Death #28	$1.95
☐ 40-905-2 Final Death #29	$1.75
☐ 40-110-8 Mugger Blood #30	$1.50
☐ 40-907-9 Head Men #31	$1.75
☐ 40-908-7 Killer Chromosomes #32	$1.75
☐ 40-909-5 Voodoo Die #33	$1.75
☐ 40-156-6 Chained Reaction #34	$1.50
☐ 41-250-9 Last Call #35	$1.95
☐ 40-912-5 Power Play #36	$1.75
☐ 41-252-5 Bottom Line #37	$1.95
☐ 40-160-4 Bay City Blast #38	$1.50
☐ 41-254-1 Missing Link #39	$1.95
☐ 40-714-9 Dangerous Games #40	$1.75
☐ 40-715-7 Firing Line #41	$1.75
☐ 40-716-5 Timber Line #42	$1.95
☐ 40-717-3 Midnight Man #43	$1.95
☐ 40-718-1 Balance of Power #44	$1.95
☐ 40-719-X Spoils of War #45	$1.95

Canadian orders must be paid with U.S. Bank check or U.S. Postal money order only.

Buy them at your local bookstore or use this handy coupon.

Clip and mail this page with your order

PINNACLE BOOKS, INC.—Reader Service Dept.
1430 Broadway, New York, NY 10018

Please send me the book(s) I have checked above. I am enclosing $_____ (please add 75¢ to cover postage and handling). Send check or money order only—no cash or C.O.D.'s.

Mr./Mrs./Miss _____

Address _____

City _____ State/Zip _____

Please allow six weeks for delivery. Prices subject to change without notice.

The Destroyer

FREE POSTER OFFER!

A full-color, 16 by 20 inch limited edition poster, reprinted from an original painting by Hector Garrido, can be yours—absolutely free—simply by sending your name and address, plus $2.50 to help defray the cost of postage and handling.

Clip and mail this page with your order

PINNACLE BOOKS, INC.—Reader Service Dept
1430 Broadway, New York, NY 10018

Please send me the free poster described above. I am enclosing $2.50 to cover postage and handling. Send check or money order only— no cash or C.O.D.'s.

Mr./Mrs./Miss _____

Address _____

City _____ State/Zip_____

Canadian orders must be paid with U.S. Bank check or U.S. Postal money order only.

Offer expires June 30, 1982. Void where prohibited by law.
Please allow 8 weeks for delivery.

the EXECUTIONER by Don Pendleton

Relax... and enjoy more of America's #1 bestselling action/adventure series!
Over 25 million copies in print!

☐ 40-737-8 War Against The Mafia #1	$1.75	☐ 40-757-2 Firebase Seattle #21	$1.75
☐ 40-738-6 Death Squad #2	$1.75	☐ 40-758-0 Hawaiian Hellground #22	$1.75
☐ 40-739-4 Battle Mask #3	$1.75	☐ 40-759-9 St. Louis Showdown #23	$1.75
☐ 41-068-9 Miami Massacre #4	$1.95	☐ 40-760-2 Canadian Crisis #24	$1.75
☐ 41-069-7 Continental Contract #5	$1.95	☐ 41-089-1 Colorado Kill-Zone #25	$1.95
☐ 40-742-4 Assault On Soho #6	$1.75	☐ 40-762-9 Acapulco Rampage #26	$1.75
☐ 41-071-9 Nightmare In New York #7	$1.95	☐ 40-763-7 Dixie Convoy #27	$1.75
☐ 40-744-0 Chicago Wipeout #8	$1.75	☐ 40-764-5 Savage Fire #28	$1.75
☐ 41-073-5 Vegas Vendetta #9	$1.95	☐ 40-765-3 Command Strike #29	$1.75
☐ 40-746-7 Caribbean Kill #10	$1.75	☐ 41-094-8 Cleveland Pipeline #30	$1.95
☐ 40-747-5 California Hit #11	$1.75	☐ 40-767-X Arizona Ambush #31	$1.75
☐ 40-748-3 Boston Blitz #12	$1.75	☐ 41-096-4 Tennessee Smash #32	$1.95
☐ 40-749-1 Washington I.O.U. #13	$1.75	☐ 41-097-2 Monday's Mob #33	$1.95
☐ 40-750-5 San Diego Siege #14	$1.75	☐ 40-770-X Terrible Tuesday #34	$1.75
☐ 40-751-3 Panic In Philly #15	$1.75	☐ 41-099-9 Wednesday's Wrath #35	$1.95
☐ 41-080-8 Sicilian Slaughter #16	$1.95	☐ 40-772-6 Thermal Thursday #36	$1.75
☐ 40-753-X Jersey Guns #17	$1.75	☐ 41-101-4 Friday's Feast #37	$1.95
☐ 40-754-8 Texas Storm #18	$1.75	☐ 40-338-0 Satan's Sabbath #38	$1.75
☐ 40-755-6 Detroit Deathwatch #19	$1.75		
☐ 40-756-4 New Orleans Knockout #20	$1.75		

Canadian orders must be paid with U.S. Bank check or U.S. Postal money order only.

Buy them at your local bookstore or use this handy coupon.

Clip and mail this page with your order

◎ **PINNACLE BOOKS, INC.—Reader Service Dept.**
1430 Broadway, New York, NY 10018

Please send me the book(s) I have checked above. I am enclosing $_____ (please add 75¢ to cover postage and handling). Send check or money order only—no cash or C.O.D.'s.

Mr./Mrs./Miss _____

Address _____

City _____ State/Zip _____

Please allow six weeks for delivery. Prices subject to change without notice.